D0981553

SHADOW WALTZ

ALSO BY AMY PATRICIA MEADE

Million Dollar Baby
Ghost of a Chance

A Marjorie McClelland Mystery

SHADOW WALTZ

AMY PATRICIA MEADE

FIRST EDITION
First Printing, 2008

Book design by Donna Burch
Cover design and image by Ellen Dahl

Midnight Ink, an imprint of Llewellyn Publications

Library of Congress Cataloging-in-Publication Data
Meade, Amy Patricia, 1972–
Shadow waltz : a Marjorie McClelland mystery / Amy Patricia Meade.—1st ed.
p. cm.
ISBN 978-0-7387-1249-9
1. McClelland, Marjorie (Fictitious character)—Fiction. 2. Women novelists—Connecticut—Fiction. 3. Betrothal—Fiction. 4. English—United States—Fiction. 5. Nineteen thirties—Fiction. 6. Women—Crimes against—Fiction. 7. Murder—Investigation—Fiction. 8. Mistresses—Fiction. I. Title.
PS3613.E128S53 2008
813'.6—dc22

2007042463

Midnight Ink
Llewellyn Publications
2143 Wooddale Drive, Dept. 978-0-7387-1249-9
Woodbury, MN 55125-2989, U.S.A.
www.midnightinkbooks.com

Printed in the United States of America

ONE

"You nearly killed her!" declared the desiccated man, his voice rising in indignation.

Creighton Ashcroft did a double take at Walter Schutt. "I beg your pardon?"

"Our Sharon. It nearly killed her when you took off the way you did," the wizened bookstore owner explained. "Without so much as a word! And then breaking off your engagement to be with the McClelland girl. It's disgraceful!"

Creighton ran a hand through his chestnut hair and heaved a loud sigh. "Mr. Schutt, Sharon and I were never engaged."

"No ring was exchanged, no, but there was an understanding."

Creighton shook his head in disbelief. To the other residents of Ridgebury, Connecticut, the year was 1935, but to Walter Schutt and his narrow frame of reference, it may as well be the turn of the century—the nineteenth century. "Understanding? We had no 'understanding.' I took her to the pictures a few times—that's all."

"You were courting her, weren't you?"

"No ... maybe ... perhaps, in a manner of speaking."

"Well, to you it may have been just speaking, but to her it was serious."

"Now see here, Mr. Schutt, I never promised Sharon anything."

The shopkeeper pulled a face. "No, young fellas like you don't promise anything, do ya? But you do your best to lead a sweet young thing like my Sharon to believe otherwise!"

The presence of the words "sweet" and "Sharon" in the same sentence made Creighton wince. "Think what you like, Mr. Schutt, but my intentions toward Sharon were never anything less than honorable. I'm sure she can verify that I never laid a finger on her." Creighton cringed again as he envisioned physical contact with the moon-faced girl.

"Even more reason for her to believe you were a gentleman." Schutt clicked his tongue chidingly. "Poor thing cried into her pillow every night for a week."

With this statement, the spherical shape of Sharon Schutt appeared from behind a curtain that divided the shop from a rear office. The girl was grinning ear-to-ear as she launched her piglike countenance into a cupcake piled high with whipped cream and topped with a maraschino cherry.

"Isn't that right, Sharon?" Schutt placed an affectionate arm around his youngest daughter.

"Hmph?" The girl questioned as crumbs streamed from her mouth.

"I told Mr. Ashcroft how you cried into your pillow every night for a week after he left."

"Huh?" Sharon answered distractedly between chews, her gaze never once moving from the partially consumed treat in her hand.

"You cried, my blossom," Schutt repeated loudly. "Every night. Remember?"

Sharon paused, obviously debating whether or not she should answer before taking another bite. "Yes," she stated flatly. "I was devastated." She turned her eyes briefly toward Creighton and bit, viciously, into the cupcake.

"I'm sorry, Sharon. I never meant to hurt you," the Englishman apologized. "But let's look on the bright side: this situation hasn't seemed to have affected your appetite. That's a good sign!" He flashed a radiant smile.

Schutt sneered. "That's only just returned this week. Until then she wouldn't eat a bite. Mrs. Schutt and I were very worried about her. Wasting away, she was!"

Creighton surveyed Sharon's corpulent figure and estimated that it would require several months of fasting before she was in any danger of "wasting away." Given Schutt's current attitude, however, he thought it best to refrain from stating so. "I thought you looked rather … um … *svelte*."

The Schutts glared at him.

"Well, as it appears I'm no longer welcome here, why don't we get down to business? I believe you have a book for Miss McClelland. May I have it please?"

Schutt scowled and reluctantly pulled a book down from the shelf behind him. "Seventy-five cents."

As Sharon returned her attention to the cupcake, Creighton hurriedly counted out the proper change and placed it on the counter, eagerly anticipating his freedom.

The bookseller eyed the three quarters on the counter and handed the book to the Englishman. However, before Creighton could get his fingers on it, Schutt pulled it back with a quick flick of the wrist. “You know, if the economy were better, I wouldn’t sell this book to Miss McClelland. Why, on principle, I shouldn’t sell it. After all, she’s just as guilty in this as you are!”

“Guilty!” Creighton sputtered. “Guilty? Why, my good man, don’t you see that she’s the victim in this whole thing? The truth is Marjorie only broke off the engagement with Detective Jameson because she found out he had his eye on some other young woman. Marjorie was desolate. Desolate!”

Where, why, or how the farfetched story had formed in his fevered brain, Creighton had no idea. He had once heard of men who had faked their own deaths to escape from prison, debts, and clinging wives and could only imagine that the same desperate state of mind was causing this spate of lies to exit from his lips. But whatever the cause, the ship had been launched and Creighton had little choice but to steer it to the next harbor.

Sharon, in the meantime, had allowed the remainder of her cupcake to drop to the floor with a soft *plop*. “Some other young woman?” she quizzed, a dab of whipped cream on her nose and her eyes agog with excitement.

“That’s not how Detective Jameson tells it,” Schutt challenged.

“Of course not,” Creighton agreed. “What man likes to admit he’s wrong?”

Schutt was stoic. “He’s a man of the law. Fine. Upstanding.” He folded his arms across his chest. “I don’t believe it.”

“Fine and upstanding have nothing to do with impressing a girl or her parents. Parents ...” Creighton’s eyes lit up. “Say, Jameson has been to your house for dinner more than once over the past few weeks hasn’t he?”

Sharon tittered breathlessly, hopped on one foot and waved her hands in the air as if stricken by some bizarre seizure.

"He has been to our house for dinner," Schutt mused. "And he did ask for a second helping of Louise's rhubarb pie. I've never seen anyone do that. I find it only tolerable myself." Lost in thought, and the prospect of marrying off his seemingly ineligible daughter, he dropped the book he had been clutching so tightly onto the counter.

Creighton snatched it up and tucked it beneath his lightweight summer suit jacket. "Why don't you invite him for dinner, Daddy?" Sharon requested. "I can make a peach pie. You know everyone loves my peach pie ..."

With that, Creighton snuck out the door of the bookstore and onto the Ridgebury village green.

TWO

Tap, tap, tap, tap! The knocks fell upon the front door in rapid succession.

Marjorie McClelland paused from typing and sighed at the page of words that had been flowing so effortlessly from her shiny new 1935 Remington typewriter. *If I don't answer, maybe they'll go away…*

Her wish was met with another series of raps—louder and more urgent than the first set and this time mingled with the piercing wail of a young child.

Marjorie quickly combed her hair with her fingers and hastened to the door. The woman standing upon the doorstep was approximately twenty years old, slight of build, and she looked as if she hadn't slept in days. "Miss McClelland?" she inquired as she tucked a wisp of dark hair behind one ear and rocked the screaming toddler in her arms.

"Yes. May I help you?"

"Oh, I hope so!" she exclaimed. "I certainly hope so! I don't know who else to turn to."

Marjorie searched the young woman's face suspiciously, but sympathy, as usual, won out over common sense. "Come in," she replied and beckoned toward the living room.

The young woman nodded and took a spot on an overstuffed floral sofa. She balanced her son upon one knee and placed a protective arm around him, but the youngster continued to cry.

"May I get you something? Some water? Something for the baby?" Marjorie offered as she smoothed the skirt of her navy blue polka-dot dress.

"No, thank you. I've already intruded upon you enough."

"Don't be silly. You've piqued my curiosity."

"I'm sorry, I didn't mean to be so dramatic. I should've at least told you my name." She leaned toward the armchair Marjorie now occupied and offered a gloved hand. "I'm Elizabeth Barnwell. And this is my son, Michael Jr."

Marjorie grasped her hand in warm welcome and smiled sweetly at the little boy. "Hello, Michael. You're not having a good day, are you?"

"Neither of us are." Elizabeth's brown eyes brimmed with tears. "You see, my husband—Michael Sr.—has been missing for two days now, and I need your help."

"My help?"

"Yes, I remember reading something about you in the papers a few months back. I know you were involved in a case since then, but the one I remember was a missing person's case just like mine."

Ah, the Van Allen affair, Marjorie mused. It seemed so long ago. Since then, she had been involved in the Nussbaum case and, her reputation as a professional sleuth established, she had been asked by local townspeople to help locate all manner of things, from runaway cats to misplaced spectacles. One enthusiastic college professor had even invited her to France to participate in a hunt for the legendary Holy Grail. Marjorie was tempted, but declined after Creighton informed her that the professor's interest in her was spurred, not so much by academic esteem, as by the full-length photograph that accompanied the article:

"Darling, you're joking! Calling the Holy Grail the 'Hilly Girl' and then saying he wanted to leave from London, fly directly to Brest, and then move south toward the Pyrenees? I hate to tell you, but I don't think he's interested in your mind..."

She shook her head and turned her attention back to the young woman on the sofa. "Mrs. Barnwell, I would love to help you, but I'm a writer, not a detective. The Van Allen case was a fluke and the Nussbaum case—well, I got involved in it strictly by chance. Now, I suggest you go home and call the police. Explain your problem to them. They—"

"I have called the police," she interjected. Michael responded to his mother's change in tone with a loud scream. "They told me this sort of thing happens all the time. 'Lots of men need a break from their old ladies,' they said. 'He'll be back before you know it,' they said. But he's never done this before, Miss McClelland. It's not like Michael..." Her voice broke into sobs.

Marjorie rose to search for a clean handkerchief but was interrupted by the sound of the front door swinging open. "Hullo, darling! Boy, do you owe me—oh, I'm sorry. I didn't realize you had company."

"It's all right, Creighton. Mrs. Barnwell, this is my associate, Mr. Creighton Ashcroft." The writer took the screaming child from his mother's lap and gathered him into her arms. "Mrs. Barnwell's husband is missing."

Creighton stepped forward and handed her the handkerchief from his front suit pocket. "I'm terribly sorry, Mrs. Barnwell. Is there anything we can do?"

"Yes, you can help me find Michael." She blew her nose loudly. "That's why I came to Miss McClelland. I remembered seeing the two of you in the papers—about your being detectives and all." She dabbed her eyes with the handkerchief and smiled at Marjorie, who held a now sleeping Michael Jr. "Oh, you have a way with children, Miss McClelland. A natural mother."

Creighton's blue eyes twinkled. "Yes, Marjorie's very maternal. Why, on many occasions, I, myself, have fought the urge to rest my head on her breast and call her 'Mother.'"

Marjorie narrowed her eyes in defiance, but she could not suppress a bit of a grin. "And many times I've wanted to spank you and send you to your room," she rallied before looking at the child in her arms. Her gaze automatically softened. "Poor dear. He has no idea of what's going on."

"That's why I came to you for help," Elizabeth spoke up. "You're a woman. I knew you'd understand. We sense things that men would normally dismiss."

Marjorie took a deep breath. However emotional Mrs. Barnwell might be, she had a good point. Men had always dismissed Marjorie's sense of intuition, however accurate it might be. Even her former beau, Detective Robert Jameson, had taken little heed of her warnings regarding the Van Allen case. The only man who had ever considered her as something more than a hysterical female was her father. Her father and Creighton.

Marjorie flashed her fiancé a proud smile before replying to Elizabeth Barnwell. "All right, we'll take the case. We'll take the case and do what we can to find your husband. But first, we need more information. What does your husband look like? What does he do for a living? Where does he go in his spare time? Did you two have an argument before he disappeared? Does he have friends or family with whom he might be staying?"

Elizabeth's face brightened. She leaned forward in her seat and answered Marjorie's questions as if by rote. "I'm afraid I don't have a photo of Michael, but he's twenty-four years old, about six feet tall, very thin, has dark hair, dark eyes, and a mustache. He works as a clerk for an insurance company. He takes the seven o'clock train to work every morning and then comes home by six for dinner and to help me put the baby to bed. He's devoted to little Michael. That's how I know something's wrong."

"And he never goes out? Not even for a drink with the boys?"

"He's not a drinking man, but he does play poker on Tuesdays and Thursdays. I don't know who he plays with or where. That's his business. I asked him once, but that's what he said. It was his business."

Marjorie frowned. A husband who was reluctant to state his whereabouts was up to no good. Period. "And you're certain that relations between the two of you were perfectly normal? No arguments that morning or the night before? Tell me everything now, Mrs. Barnwell, because it will eventually come out."

"No. No arguments. It was a typical day. He went to work like he does every morning, but he never came home for supper that night. Even on poker nights he'd come home for supper. He always came home for supper . . ." Her voice trailed off again.

"And you noticed nothing strange about his behavior? Nothing that might help us find him?"

She dabbed her swollen eyes with a damp handkerchief and extracted a large key and scrap of paper from her purse. "I did find these. They were in the pocket of the suit he was wearing the night before he disappeared. I always check the pockets before I bring his suits to the cleaners. Bought him a Christmas present once with all the change I saved."

Creighton smiled sympathetically and took the items from Mrs. Barnwell's hand. He turned the key over and read its number aloud. "7905. Looks like a key to a safe-deposit box."

Marjorie, the sleeping child still in her arms, moved from her seat and perched on the arm of Creighton's chair. "No, I don't think so. It's too big for a safe deposit box. What's written on that scrap of paper?"

"An address and a phone number. 23 Lakeview Road. Exeter19."

"Try calling and see what you get."

"I did already," Mrs. Barnwell interjected. "No one answered."

Creighton stood up and headed toward the phone on Marjorie's desk. "Doesn't hurt to try again."

A couple of minutes and a few tries later he replaced the handset on the cradle with a loud sigh. "Still no reply. Maybe we should check out that address. The key might open something there."

Marjorie shook her head. "I know that area. Small bungalows near a lake. I can't imagine any household lock that would require a key like this. Although we should probably check it out anyway.

It might—" She turned the scrap of paper over. "Wait one minute. This is a train schedule."

"What?"

"This scrap of paper is from a train schedule."

"So?"

"So, when someone scribbles a number and address, they use the first thing they have available. In this case, Michael used a train schedule, meaning he was most likely in the train station at the time or, at the very least, had just left it. Leading us to believe that the key most likely opens something there."

Creighton grinned and held the key aloft. "Something like a locker?"

THREE

THEY ARRIVED AT HARTFORD Station at approximately two in the afternoon—well after the morning rush of suited businessmen with briefcases and well before the same men and women, shirt collars unbuttoned and ties undone, made the tiresome journey back home.

Creighton browsed the rows of industrial gray lockers until he located the one whose number matched the key. "Here we are: 7905. Although what we could possibly find in there, I haven't the foggiest notion."

Marjorie toyed with the brim of her floppy white hat distractedly. "Anything that might give us a clue as to where Michael Barnwell may have gone. Ticket stub, hotel reservation, receipts ..."

"A map with his destination clearly circled in red ink. That's what I'm hoping for at least. That way Mr. Barnwell can be reunited with his wife and son and we can go on our merry way."

Marjorie clucked her tongue. "Creighton, don't you want to be involved on this case? After all, it was your idea to help that poor girl."

"I do, but I've also been around long enough to recognize a potentially awkward domestic situation. What if we discover that Michael Barnwell has run off with his mistress? Or worse yet, has a veritable harem of girlfriends? Have you given any thought to that? Because, I, for one, don't want to be the one to break the news to her."

Marjorie frowned. "Neither do I. But she's better off finding out now than spending the rest of her life wondering and waiting. We promised we'd help her, Creighton, whatever helping her brings. Besides, I'm not sure we're going to find a harem—women can generally sense that sort of thing. We can tell when a man is lying or when he isn't telling us everything." She inserted the key into the lock and turned. "Just as well as we can tell when a man truly loves us."

Creighton scanned Marjorie's face for a trace of mockery but found none. For months, she had carried on with Detective Robert Jameson, oblivious of Creighton's ardor. Desperate to get the writer's attention, he wooed the only other unmarried female in town: moon-faced Sharon Schutt. Precisely when his simple scheme to invoke Marjorie's jealousy had evolved into full-blown courtship with Miss Schutt, he couldn't say. His relationship with the socially and aesthetically challenged Sharon was rather like a hit-and-run accident: one moment in total control of his destiny, the next, speechless and paralyzed in a garish dining room, listening to talk of new curtains, nurseries, and the virtues of molded salads. The exact moment of impact was difficult to pinpoint, but the effects of the collision—and the memory of a set of stubby, padded fingers upon his knee—were long-lasting.

"You're right. I certainly could never hide anything from you. Heaven knows, I only courted Sharon all those months so I could get more of her mother's Perfection Salad. And you dated—oh, what's his name again?"

"Robert."

"Yes," he replied, "and you dated Detective Robert Jameson just to play hard to get."

Marjorie laughed and threw her arms around Creighton's neck. "Okay, so maybe I don't always understand men. But we're engaged to be married now, aren't we?"

Creighton smiled and kissed her. "Yes we are, thank goodness. Which reminds me..."

"Yes?"

"You introduced me to Elizabeth Barnwell as your 'associate,' not your fiancé."

"It seemed more professional. More businesslike. Besides," she added, "we haven't set a date yet or made any other formal arrangements or announcements."

Creighton lifted Marjorie's left hand from behind his neck and stared at the exquisite diamond on her left ring finger. "I think this flashbulb is enough of an announcement, don't you? And I don't think a business associate would kiss you like this."

He pulled her closer, placed his lips on hers and kissed her hungrily.

Marjorie grinned afterward. "That professor searching for the 'Hilly Girl' might."

"Over my dead body," Creighton jokingly threatened. "If he had laid a finger on you, he'd have been joining those relics he collects."

"Hmmm, another mystery to solve."

"No mystery," he said. "I'd happily confess and once the men in the jury got a glimpse of you, they wouldn't dare convict me."

"Why, Mr. Ashcroft, what pugilistic tendencies you have!"

Marjorie kissed her future husband and then returned her focus to the locker. She struggled to open the door, but to no avail. "The key's in the lock, but it won't turn."

"Let me try."

She stepped aside so Creighton could try his hand; however, he also met with no success. "Hmph," he grunted. "We're obviously on the wrong track. This key must open something else."

"But what?" She pulled a face.

"I don't know, but it's not this locker. I'm disappointed, but I can't say I'm surprised. Railway station lockers are rather clichéd these days."

"Clichéd?"

"Yes. Lately it seems every film out of Hollywood and every mystery novel contains a railway station locker filled with money, government documents, or some other ill-gotten gains."

"Not my books," Marjorie stated proudly.

"That's because you are, Marjorie, if nothing else, unpredictable." He gave her a peck on the cheek and then removed the key from the locker and stared at it. "And so, I'm happy to say, is Michael Barnwell."

"Happy? I thought you wanted to find a map with his location circled in red."

"I did, for his family's sake." He draped an arm casually around Marjorie's shoulder, and the two of them strolled slowly toward the exit. "But now that we're embroiled in another case, I must admit that it's rather nice sleuthing with you again."

The writer stopped dead in her tracks. "Are you joking? Last time I had to drag you along, kicking and screaming. What gives?"

"Nothing. Just letting you know that you're not the only one capable of being unpredictable."

Marjorie waved her hand dismissively.

He grinned and continued. "Besides, I'm too tired to argue with you."

"You, tired? What do you have to be tired from?"

"Lots. You think it's easy being witty and charming all the time?"

Marjorie rolled her eyes. "Just think how tired you'd be if you were actually good at it."

Creighton arched a chestnut brown eyebrow. "Yes. Too tired to drive to Lakeview Road for starters …"

The statement had the desired effect. Marjorie nearly leapt into his arms. "Oh Creighton! Are you serious? Can we go there now? Please!"

He feigned a weary sigh and pulled the brim of his gray Homburg jauntily over one eye. "Anything for you, Marjorie. Anything for you."

FOUR

CREIGHTON PULLED HIS 1929 Rolls Royce Phantom II Continental to a stop alongside the curb, exited through the driver's side door, and then assisted Marjorie out of the passenger seat.

"Well," Marjorie commented as she placed both feet upon the graded dirt road, "here goes nothing."

"Not the type of reaction I'd expect from you. We're embarking on a new case. Where's your excitement? Your wide-eyed optimism?" Creighton asked as he shut the door behind her.

"I'm not any less optimistic than usual, but this place—" she shuddered "—this place gives me the creeps."

He took her hand in his and escorted her up the cracked cement walkway that led to the front door. "I know it's a bit rundown, but there's nothing about this house that strikes me as particularly sinister."

Marjorie shook her head slowly. "I don't know. Something's just gnawing at me—"

"You won't find what you're lookin' for in there," a thick brogue warned from the other side of the yard. Creighton and Marjorie spun around to find a heavyset elderly woman leaning across the dilapidated picket fence that separated the green house from the white one next door. "Ain't seen hide nor hair of no one for days."

"Who lives here?" Marjorie inquired.

"Ronnie. Ronnie Carter."

"And you say you haven't seen him in a while?" Creighton pressed.

The woman chortled and stuck her hands in the pockets of her stained blue housecoat. "Him? Ronnie ain't a 'him.' She's a 'her.' Short for 'Veronica'—a much prettier name than 'Ronnie,' but a bit too dainty, if ya please."

"Why?" Marjorie asked. "Is Ronnie a—um—big girl?"

"Ronnie? No," she sang. "Why, I could wrap my apron strings around her twice, so thin she is! But she's a bit of a tough. Aye, she knows the workin's of the world, that one. 'Tis a shame, really. She'd be a pretty lass without all that paint. If she mended her ways t'wouldn't be hard for her to find a decent husband."

Uninterested in Ronnie's marital prospects, Creighton steered the conversation back to a more relevant topic. "When was the last time you saw Miss Carter?"

"Oh, must be going on three days now. 'Twas nighttime—I remember cause I was in me dressing gown—when there came an awful ruckus from next door. Who Ronnie was arguin' with, I don't know, but it was a dreadful row. Swearin', screamin'... a right donnybrook going on. Then, all of a sudden, quiet." She punctuated this statement with a nod of the head that sent several frowsy wisps of yellowish gray hair tumbling from the loose bun at the back of her neck. "Haven't heard a whisper since."

"Why didn't you call the police, Mrs.—?" Marjorie's voice trailed off.

"Sullivan. 'Cause I don't go messin' about in other people's business."

"Other people's business?" Creighton quizzed. "How could you be certain that this young woman wasn't being robbed or assaulted?"

"'Cause," Mrs. Sullivan leaned in close and lowered her voice, "between you, me, and the Lord Almighty, Ronnie's a bit of a 'fast one.' Has people coming here at all hours. Some even stay the night, if you catch me meanin'. If she were screamin', it was likely 'cause one boyfriend found out about another and gave her a proper thrashing for it. Can't say I'd blame 'im either."

"How long has Ronnie lived here?"

"About four months now," Mrs. Sullivan narrowed her eyes, the pleasure of a day's gossip giving way to suspicion. "And now that I've answered your questions, supposin' you tell me who you are and why you're so interested in Ronnie."

Creighton tipped his hat and bowed slightly. "My pleasure. My name is Creighton Ashcroft and this is my fiancée, Marjorie McClelland. We're private detectives. Perhaps you read about us in the papers?"

"I don't have time to read the papers—not since Mr. Sullivan passed on anyways. I earn me livin' at the lunchroom in the plant across town and when I'm not there, I'm busy keeping this place spic-and-span." She thrust a thumb toward the tidy white cottage behind her. "I may be poor, but that don't mean I've got to live in filth."

Mrs. Sullivan's eyes turned toward Marjorie and a grin spread across her face. "Your name's McClelland, is it? Then you'll be knowin' how proud we micks are. If you don't mind me askin', what part of Ireland is your family from?"

"County Antrim, I think," Marjorie replied.

"Ah, should have known it by looking at ya. Why, your eyes are as green as old Erin herself, don't you know." The old woman smiled appraisingly and then slid her eyes toward Creighton. "Marrying an Englishman, eh? Well, I suppose that's what the world's comin' to isn't it? People marryin' whoever they please, with no regard for God or family. And runnin' 'round as private detectives, no less. Not that I've known any private detectives in my time, mind you. Though I've seen 'em in the cinema, and I do like that William Powell. He's not like me Mr. Sullivan, God rest his soul—no dirt under his fingernails, if you please—but I do love his mustache and his cheek. No, I can't say that I'd much mind having his slippers under me bed!" She chuckled loudly and then grew serious. "Ronnie isn't in any trouble is she? She's no better than she ought to be, mind you, but I'd hate to see her in a bad spot."

"We don't know," Creighton answered honestly. "We were asked to track a missing person and were led to this address."

"Hmmm," the woman mused. "I'm supposin' this person who's missin' is a gentleman?"

Creighton smiled at the old woman's perception. "Yes, he is. His name is Michael Barnwell. Mid-twenties, tall, dark, and has a mustache."

"Sounds like the fella who's been hangin' about here as of late."

"I thought there were a lot of 'fellas' hanging about here," Creighton challenged.

"And so there have been, but this one you're describin' was different, that's why I remembered him. Wore a suit, he did, and always carryin' a case—not like the riffraff that's usually paradin' around this place."

"When was the last time you saw him?" Marjorie asked.

"The night before that big fight I told you 'bout. I was walkin' home from the plant and he was standin' right there," she pointed at the door of the green cottage. "Must have had a key, 'cause he didn't ring the bell. He let himself right in."

"And the next day was the last time you saw Ronnie?" Marjorie sought clarification.

"Yes ... well, no. I can't say I saw her, but I heard her screamin'. Half the neighborhood did."

"When was the last time you did see her?"

"Ah, a week or so before then, maybe more."

Marjorie and Creighton exchanged glances and nods.

"Well, thank you, Mrs. Sullivan," Creighton stated gratefully. "You've been a great help. If we need anything else, would it be all right if we called upon you again?"

The Irishwoman folded her arms across her ample chest and gave the Englishman a wink. "You know where to find me, darlin'," she grinned.

Mrs. Sullivan returned to her small yet tidy house, leaving Marjorie and Creighton to continue their investigation. Once the Irishwoman was safely out of earshot, Marjorie commented, "Looks like you've done wonders for Irish-English relations." Then she added, with a playful wink, "Darlin'."

"Yes, it's the same thing all the time, isn't it?" he sighed. "And I was taking it easy on the old girl. Just imagine what would have happened had I revealed my rapier-sharp wit." He removed his hat and smoothed his hair back in an exaggerated act of preening.

Marjorie shook her head and laughed.

He returned his hat to his head. "You scoff because even you haven't experienced the Ashcroft charm in its fullest. I've been holding back, because I respect you too much to transform you into a quivering gelatinous mass of passion. But rest assured, darling, if I were to unleash all of its dynamic power, you wouldn't be able to keep your hands off me." With a deft motion, he grabbed Marjorie around the waist and drew her close to him. "However, if you don't believe me, I'd be more than willing to demonstrate."

Marjorie pulled Creighton's hat down over his eyes and gently pushed him away. "Put your rapier back in its scabbard. We have more important things to do right now." She strolled slowly toward the front door of the cottage.

Creighton fixed his hat, a twinkle in his eye. "You're a strong woman, Marjorie McClelland. But just you wait until our wedding night; you won't be able to resist so easily then."

"I'm looking forward to the challenge," she purred over one shoulder. "So long as you don't become another Michael Barnwell."

Creighton frowned. "No, it seems he isn't quite the devoted family man his wife made him out to be."

Marjorie shook her head slowly. "I feel awfully sorry for Elizabeth, but I can't say I'm surprised. When a man won't tell you his whereabouts, he's up to no good."

"You know, darling, your wisdom regarding the opposite sex is simply astounding. First, you're certain Michael Barnwell is faithful because 'women can sense those things.' Now, 'you knew all along that he was up to no good.' Why, you're so insightful, it's amazing we didn't get together sooner. Oh wait!" He emphasized the utterance with the snap of his fingers. "You were engaged to Detective Jameson, weren't you? That must be why you couldn't perceive my ardor—your talents were being utilized to peer into the boundless depths of your former beau: a man who subscribes to *Junior Detective* magazine and whose favorite color is brown. Yes, that's it. If you hadn't been so consumed with Jameson, I'm sure you would have sensed my true feelings. After all, compared with the complex personality of the detective, I must seem a very easy nut to crack."

Marjorie clicked her tongue and suppressed a laugh. "Tsk, tsk, tsk. Are you still carrying on about that? If I didn't know better, I'd say someone was still jealous."

Truth be told, the knowledge that Jameson's lips had once touched Marjorie's was more than a bit nettlesome, but Creighton would rather die than admit it, lest his fiancée hold it over his head the remainder of his life. "Not at all. I've won the heart, and hand, of fair maiden. Besides," he added, recalling the exchange he had in the bookshop that morning, "it won't be long before some other girl comes along to knock Jameson off his feet."

"I think you mean 'sweep' him off his feet."

"No, darling, in this case I'm certain I mean 'knock.'" He cleared his throat awkwardly and climbed the few steps to the front door of the bungalow. "Which is exactly what I'm about to do to this door." He raised his hand and let it fall upon the whitewashed wooden entrance. The action not only made a loud rapping sound, but caused the door to creak slowly inward.

Marjorie gripped Creighton's arm in tense anticipation. "Do you think we should go in?"

"I don't see why not." He pushed the door ajar and took a step forward.

Marjorie tugged him back. "I'm not sure we should be doing this. What if we get caught? We could be charged with breaking and entering or trespassing or … or worse!"

Creighton narrowed his eyes. "What happened to Marjorie McClelland, fearless fact-finding femme fatale?"

"She's alive and well, thank you very much!" She cast her eyes downward and poked at the cement of the front stoop with the toe of her shoe. "But I was thinking that maybe I should be a bit more … responsible … cautious …"

"Cautious? You thrive on excitement and intrigue, so, as you put it earlier, what gives?"

"I'm scared," she answered reluctantly. "All right? There, I said it. Are you happy?"

"Scared? I don't believe it! You wanted to come here and, despite your protests to the contrary, you do want to see what's behind that door."

"Yes … yes, I do, but I have a very bad feeling about all of this. Something just isn't right."

"What do you think is wrong?"

Marjorie bit her lip in contemplation. "I don't know. I don't even know that there is something wrong." She shook her head and sighed heavily. "Oh, I'm being ridiculous. Probably all that time with Robert."

Creighton turned up his nose and nodded. "Dreadfully unadventurous, wasn't he?"

Marjorie didn't answer. Regaining possession of herself, she pushed past Creighton, fiddled with the lock, and swung the door open wide. "Let's go!" she added as she jerked her head toward the entrance.

"That's my g—" Before Creighton could complete the sentence, Marjorie grabbed him by the arm and dragged him indoors.

The interior of the cottage was dim, but their eyesight quickly adjusted to the weak lighting.

"It's empty," Marjorie declared as she surveyed the vacant living room.

The ventilation from the open door sent dust balls scurrying across the hardwood floor like tumbleweeds.

Creighton scanned the walls, noting the darker areas where pictures once hung against the nicotine-stained, yellow-tinted plaster. "Miss Carter is a smoker," he noted.

Marjorie nodded in agreement. "Mmm. My father smoked a pipe, and when I washed the windows twice a year, they were nearly brown." Her green eyes widened. "I know it's quite the fashion, but no matter how I tried, I never could get the hang of smoking."

Creighton smirked. No matter how intelligent, brave, or worldly Marjorie managed to appear, there remained, beneath her imperturbable surface, a naïve little girl. "I don't think you're cut out for tobacco, darling."

"No, I suppose not." She pulled a face. "Although sometimes I see a film with Jean Harlow or Mae West and I wonder . . ."

Creighton stepped forward and kissed his future wife on the forehead. "Well, stop wondering. The only person I ever want you to be is you."

Marjorie giggled and threw her arms about his neck and then looked up suddenly. "What's that dripping sound?"

He brushed his lips lightly against her hair and moved into the kitchen. "Leaky tap," he called from the vacant cooking area. "Looks as if Ronnie had a penchant for frying. There's a pan full of grease on the stove." He opened and closed the icebox doors and those of the grease-splattered cupboards. "Nothing here but bacon grease, bread crumbs, and—oh, wait a tick."

Marjorie joined him in the kitchen, where a set of personalized luggage sat by the back door waiting for an eager traveler to snatch them up and tote them to some exotic locale.

He bent down over the slightly tattered suitcases. "V.C.," he read aloud. "At one time Veronica Carter had money."

"No," Marjorie argued. "Those are cheap knockoffs. Mrs. Patterson and I saw a set at Fox's Department Store just like it when we were shopping for my trousseau. The monogramming was free and you had the option of buying them on time."

"Fascinating, but it still doesn't tell us what happened to Ronnie Carter. Or why she left her luggage behind." Creighton popped the spring mechanism on one of the cases only to find it empty. He continued to pry the remaining two lids ajar. Again, all they contained was air.

"One is missing," Marjorie noted.

"How do you know?"

"Because the ones I saw were sold in a set of four and they were graduated in size. The smallest is a train case for makeup and toiletries. The next biggest is a valise—it's used for short overnight stays. That big one," she tapped it with the toe of her right foot, "is about two and a half times the size of the valise and for lengthy trips. But there's supposed to be a case in between the two. Something that the average woman could take along for a week away, say to Niagara Falls for a honeymoon?"

"I don't think Veronica was going on a honeymoon, hanging about the likes of Michael Barnwell." He grinned from ear to ear. "And as for our honeymoon, my dear, considering what I have planned, the valise would be quite adequate." He ended the statement with a wiggle of his eyebrows.

Marjorie mimicked the gesture but quickly regained momentum. "Sounds lovely, but at the moment, we're faced with the matter of a missing suitcase."

"Simple. Veronica 'Ronnie' Carter packed her things into it and ran away with Michael Barnwell. Case solved."

"The case isn't solved. We haven't a shred of evidence to support your theory and I, for one, would like some cold, hard facts before I tell a poor young mother that her husband has run off with another woman."

Creighton bit his bottom lip in thoughtful silence. "I would too, but we can make some pretty strong assumptions."

"Assumptions? All we have to go on is Mrs. Sullivan's story, an empty house, and a piece of luggage that may or may not be missing. That leaves a lot of holes, not the least of which is the matter of this key." She raised the small metallic object in the air. "Is it important to this case? And, if so, what does it open?"

"Is it for the front door?"

"No, I checked it on the way in."

"And," Creighton stepped back and examined the back kitchen door, "it's not for this either. But we still haven't checked the rest of the house."

Marjorie nodded and proceeded down the dark narrow passage that connected the living room and kitchen to the remainder of the bungalow. The hallway—if one could call it that, for it was all of twelve feet long—contained three doorways of varying size. Marjorie grabbed the handle of the door to her immediate right and turned it until it clicked. The door swung inward to reveal a medium-sized, square room whose only contents were a bare mattress and a small lamp with no shade.

Creighton walked around the perimeter of the bed and scanned the floor. "Nothing here," he remarked before he stepped back into the hallway.

Marjorie joined him and selected the narrow door at the end of the hall as the next area to investigate. She was disappointed to find an empty linen closet. "Two down, one to go," she commented as she directed Creighton to the last unexplored door.

He pushed it open, exposing a small closetlike space lined with cracked white ceramic tiles. To the left stood a small pedestal sink, beside it an old-fashioned pull-chain toilet, and, against the far wall, beneath an open window, a cast-iron bathtub sporting peeling paint and a reddish-brown circle around the drain.

Creighton twisted the cold-water tap of the sink, causing the pipes to bang loudly and a rust-colored substance to ooze from the faucet. He grimaced and quickly turned the tap back to the right. "Even a jigger of scotch won't help that."

Marjorie, meanwhile, was checking the medicine cabinet.

"Find anything?"

"A broken eyelash curler, a stub of styptic pencil, and an empty bottle of Evening in Paris," she answered and closed the door of the cabinet abruptly.

"Hardly the sort of discovery that will crack the case wide open."

"No, but maybe ..." her eyes grew wild as she stepped onto the toilet seat.

Creighton recognized that familiar gleam. "Oh no, what have you thought of now?"

"I remember—" her words started and stopped as she strained to reach the top of the tank. "I—was—paging through—one of—ugh—one of Robert's detective magazines—and there was a story—about—oof—some gangster—who—hid—something—important—on top of—one—of—these."

"What was it?"

She felt along the top of the tank with her fingertips. "I—don't—remember. Guns—bootleg—whiskey—something."

"Ah. Umm, darling? That doesn't look very sturdy. Why don't you step on the lid instead of the, er ... ?"

"There—isn't—one—oh!" No sooner had she answered than her right foot slipped off the seat and dangled ominously over the bowl of rusty water below. Thrown completely off balance, she waved one arm while clawing frantically at the tank with the other.

Creighton stared, open-mouthed and helpless at the silent, frenetic ballet before moving into position behind his fiancée. "Marjorie," he shouted. "Don't worry, I've got—"

"Aaaaaahhhhhh," she wailed as she teetered back and forth upon her porcelain perch. Instinctively, she reached out for something with which to steady herself and was relieved when her fingers met with cold metal.

The relief was short-lived, however, for the object did nothing to help her regain her balance. Instead, it moved beneath her grasp and seemed to be growing longer.

The chain.

Marjorie felt herself falling backward toward the hard tile wall. She closed her eyes and braced herself for the worst.

"Marjorie," Creighton ordered as he positioned himself behind her. "Let go of—!"

Creighton's words were drowned out by a loud *ploop* followed by a resounding *whoosh*. Cold water rushed against her right ankle.

She opened her eyes to find that her torso was safely cradled in Creighton's arms, but her foot was wedged firmly in the siphon part of the bowl. She struggled to pull herself free, but the suction created by the flush, as well as the increasing pressure caused by the cascade of fresh, albeit rust-tinged, water made it impossible.

"I'm stuck! Oh Creighton, help!"

Creighton obediently let Marjorie's left leg drop to the floor and then, placing a hand under each of her arms, braced himself against the wall. "All right, on the count of three, pull! Ready? One . . . two . . . three . . . go!"

The couple pulled as hard as they could, grunting and groaning with every tug, yet, despite all their efforts, the only visible results were Marjorie's dress being yanked to scandalous heights, Creighton being pinned, by an overzealous Marjorie, against the wall, and an ever-expanding pool of murky water on the floor.

"It's no use," he sighed. "We're going to have to remove your shoe."

"Oh no! I love these shoes."

"Well, it's either you or the shoes, darling."

"There's no other way to get my foot out of there?"

"There is, but I don't think you want me summoning the Hartford Fire Department to get your foot out of a loo."

"Not particularly," she pouted. "Go ahead and take the shoe off."

"Me?" he nearly shouted. "It was your idea to stand up there, and it's your shoe."

"Please," she pleaded. "That water is so—so—brown."

"Mmm, right up Jameson's alley. Too bad he isn't here to lend a hand."

Marjorie sulked as she smoothed her dress into place.

Creighton chuckled. "You needn't bother. Any enjoyment I might derive from the sight of your bare thigh is mitigated by what's at the other end of your calf."

She placed her hands on her hips and thrust her nose into the air. Water continued to stream onto the tile floor.

Creighton laughed even harder. "Only you could manage to get caught in such an absurd situation. And only you could still try to look dignified with your foot in a—well, a crapper." Still chuckling, he removed his jacket, slung it over the bathroom door, and proceeded to roll up his sleeves.

Marjorie jolted to life. "What are you doing?"

"You know precisely what I'm doing. I'm taking off your shoe."

"Oh thank you, Creighton! You're so good to me."

He bent down, dipped one hand into the rusty water and pulled it out again. "Anything for you, my dear. Anything . . ." He scrutinized the flesh of his palm, grimaced "... for..." and then plunged it back into the bowl "... you."

It took Creighton thirty minutes to extricate Marjorie from her watery captivity.

She immediately leaned against the tiled bathroom wall and massaged her sore foot. The tops of her toes were bruised and a red line marked where the vamp of her shoe had dug into the metatarsal area. "Whew, that's much better. Now all I need is my shoe and—hey, where'd my shoe go?"

Creighton pointed at the siphon. "Down there."

"No, there has to be a way to get it back. What about a plunger?"

"Did you see any?"

Marjorie shook her head.

"Neither did I," he continued. "But what's even worse than the loss of your shoe is that if we don't find a way to shut the water off, this place will be flooded." Creighton bent down and, reaching behind the bowl, grabbed a small, rusty valve. "This should do it," he announced.

He knelt down and attempted to push the regulating device to the left. Marjorie watched admiringly as the muscles in her fiancé's forearm tightened and tensed as he utilized more and more strength in the endeavor. Flakes of corroded metal yielded to the pressure and sprinkled downward; however, the valve still held firmly.

"Rusted through," he declared as he rose to his feet. "There has to be a main shutoff somewhere. Did you happen to see a cellar door?"

"No. Well, not inside at least. Perhaps out back."

They retreated back down the hallway, through the kitchen and out the back door, Marjorie hobbling the whole way on one shoe and one bare foot.

"Aha!" Creighton exclaimed as he stepped down onto the dilapidated brick stoop.

Marjorie followed his gaze to a set of metal Bilco doors, fastened with a shiny steel padlock. Forgetting her semi-shod state, she bounded excitedly down the steps, twisting her ankle in the process.

"Careful, sweetheart," he warned.

She paid no heed to the tinge of pain in her foot but went directly to the lock. "7905," she said aloud as she read the serial number etched below the keyhole. "Well, that answers that question." She passed the key to Creighton. "Here, you open it. You're the plumber."

He took the key, inserted it into the lock and turned it. The lock sprung open with minimal effort. "Strange that Barnwell should have a key for the cellar in his pocket."

Marjorie shrugged. "Maybe he had to do the same thing you're doing."

"Turn off the water because Veronica got her foot stuck in a—?"

"I meant," she interrupted, "fix the plumbing."

"Ah, right," he said with a nod and a wink. He bent down, grasped the handle of the topmost door, opened it, and then repeated the process with the second, exposing a set of subterranean stairs.

The stairway, however, wasn't the only thing to emerge into the daylight, for as the couple pulled the doors back, a horrible odor rose to the surface. Marjorie covered her nose with her hands.

Creighton stepped forward and, placing an arm around her shoulders, shielded her nose and mouth with a monogrammed handkerchief.

"Oh Creighton! What is that?"

"Probably a dead mouse," he asserted.

"A dead mouse? You haven't been in Connecticut very long have you? The only way a mouse could make a stink like that is if it were eighty pounds and four feet long."

He pulled a face. "No, you're right. Here, hold this," he handed her the handkerchief. "I'll go down to take a look."

Marjorie leapt forward, letting the handkerchief fall to the ground. "Oh no, Creighton! I don't want you going down there by yourself."

He held her close and stroked her hair soothingly. "No, Marjorie. You wait here. It's probably just stagnant water from a leaky pipe."

She drew him close and buried her face in his shoulder. "You know it's not a leak either."

"I know better than to try to shield you, darling, but just trust me this time. Go to the car and wait there."

"No, I want to stay with you. Besides, I've come this far. I want to see this through to the end—dead mouse, stagnant water, or otherwise."

Creighton sighed wearily. "All right. Come on, but let's grab a flashlight first."

They went to the front of the house where the Phantom was parked. Through an open window of the bungalow, they could see Mrs. Sullivan keeping her house "spic-and-span."

Creighton reached into the glove box and retrieved a flashlight. He tested it by flicking the on switch several times. Satisfied that the battery was strong enough for the task at hand, he nodded to Marjorie. "I'm going down there. You stay here."

"No!" she shouted. "We agreed!"

"Marjorie, you're staying here if I have to lock you in this car myself!" he boomed.

She timidly sunk bank into the passenger seat of the Phantom. Creighton strode off to the backyard. He did not enjoy utilizing such bully tactics—it wasn't in his nature—but he was willing to do whatever was necessary to ensure that she was protected.

He walked slowly down the flight of stairs, the beam of his flashlight picking out objects with every step of the journey. When he felt that he could travel no farther and that the odor was too overwhelming to be ignored, he focused the light on the floor beneath his feet. A surge of bile rushed up his throat and he might have vomited on the spot if he hadn't turned around to find Marjorie.

"Creighton," she implored as she slid her arms around his neck. "Creighton, don't be angry. I wanted to be here with you. I—" Her eyes slid to the floor of the cellar, causing her body to tense and her vocal cords to issue forth a high-pitched scream the likes of which Creighton had seldom heard before.

He held her head against his chest. "Don't look, Marjorie. Don't look . . . don't look . . ."

FIVE

Marjorie reclined upon a gurney as a middle-aged ambulance driver wrapped her foot with an elastic bandage. "Looks like a bad sprain, miss, but it should be better in a few days if you stay off of it." He displayed a reassuring smile and went back to work.

Marjorie tried hard to reciprocate, but all she could do was shiver, despite the coarse woolen blanket draped over her shoulders, and watch as uniformed policemen crawled around the property, snapping photos and placing objects in bags.

"Think we're in for rain," the ambulance driver commented.

The August day had grown overcast and a stiff breeze was blowing the leaves so that their silver undersides were visible. Marjorie nodded her reply, but it was not the weather that caused her chill as much as the featureless corpse that lay, just a few yards away, in the cellar of Veronica Carter's home.

She closed her eyes and wondered if she would ever be able to forget what she had seen.

When she opened them, she saw Creighton approaching, bearing two paper cups of water and escorting two familiar gentlemen to the crime scene.

"Look who I found, waiting at the corner for a bus: Detective Jameson and Officer Noonan."

Noonan, the stereotype of the all-brawn Irish beat cop, either bore the brunt of Creighton's jokes or missed them completely. "We weren't waiting for a bus," Noonan clarified. "We drove here, in the car." He pointed to the other side of the street. "We were on duty when we got the call."

Marjorie couldn't help but smile. "Hi, Noonan. How's the wife and kids?"

Noonan performed a small bow. "Hiya. They're swell, Marjorie. How 'bout you?"

"Oh, not bad." Her eyes slid to her former beau. "Hello, Robert."

Looking as if he had just stepped off a Hollywood set, Detective Jameson had leading-man good looks that belied his small-town conservatism. He tipped his hat, struggling to avoid eye contact. "Hi, Marjorie."

Marjorie felt a pang of guilt. She knew perfectly well that had she not ended her romance with Jameson, the good detective would have been perfectly content to see it continue.

The guilt was short lived, for it was not long before Jameson started his usual annoying police-academy rhetoric. "I should have known I'd find you two here," he remarked peevishly. "What laws did you break this time?"

Marjorie sighed. She should have learned by now not to let sentimental notions overrule her intellect. "Unless you can pin the death of a mutilated corpse on us, we're in the clear."

"Really? What about unlawful entry?" He smirked. "Did you get permission to search the house?"

"From whom? The woman in the cellar?" she rallied.

Creighton and Noonan both took a step backward. They were educated enough in the science of life to realize that provoking an agitated female—particularly this agitated female—was comparable to shaving over a bad sunburn. Dealing with the first situation was bad enough. The second? Excruciating.

Jameson cleared his throat. "No, I suppose not. You say the body's mutilated?"

"Yes. If you'd stop pestering us and take a look at it, you'd know that already."

The detective threaded his fingers through the belt loops of his trousers, pulling his suit jacket back just enough to reveal a gun, fitted snugly in its holster. "With all due respect, Miss McClelland—"

"Oh, it's Miss McClelland now," Marjorie interrupted.

"—you're a civilian. Most crime scenes are too violent for your, well, feminine sensibilities. Noonan and I, however—" He gestured to his partner, who was adamantly waving his hands while mouthing the word "No."

"Noonan and I, however," Jameson repeated while shooting the officer a stern look, "are trained professionals. There's very little we haven't seen."

"Oh?" Marjorie thrust her chin out defiantly. Hartford was a large town—the capital of Connecticut—but it was hardly a hotbed of crime. Aside from the Van Allen and Nussbaum cases, the only incident she could recall that was as violent in nature as this involved a man who had lost an arm while driving, at high speed, through a tollbooth. The precise details of the story eluded her at the moment; however, she did remember that it involved alcohol and a considerable lack of depth perception.

She was about to cite the number of times during their brief betrothal that Jameson would complain about rescuing cats out of trees or somehow let it slip that he and Noonan had spent an afternoon at the county's local Ridgebury/Exeter station, listening to boxing matches over the radio, but quickly reconsidered. "You're right. I'm certain you've encountered many corpses who've had their faces beaten in and their hands and feet cut off. Probably worse, although I, as a naïve young female, couldn't possibly imagine the many ways in which one person could murder another."

Creighton smiled proudly at his fiancée's tongue-in-cheek reply.

Jameson, meanwhile, was completely nonplussed. "You can't? But, you're a—you're a … never mind." He shook his head dismissively and headed off toward the house. "Come on, Noonan. Creighton, Marjorie," he shouted over his shoulder, "wait here. We'll need a complete statement when we get back. You know the drill."

"Yes, Detective, I know the drill," Creighton shouted back and then added, sotto voce, "it's the same one my dentist uses."

Jameson and Noonan returned a few minutes later, pale and visibly upset.

Noonan wiped his mouth with his handkerchief. "I've been with the force twenty years, and I ain't never seen anything as bad as that."

Jameson fidgeted uncomfortably with his tie. "How did you find her?"

Creighton begged the question. "We opened the Bilco doors, noticed the smell, went down to investigate, and there she was."

"I meant why are you here?"

Marjorie and Creighton exchanged glances but remained silent.

"Look," Jameson reasoned, "I don't know what you guys are up to or who you're trying to protect, but you're mixed up in some serious business. You saw what happened to that girl down there. You two want to be next? Creighton," he addressed the Englishman, "that could be Marjorie lying down there. I don't think you want to take that risk, do you?"

"That's certainly hitting below the belt," Marjorie remarked.

"It's not a jibe, it's a fact," Jameson contested. "Don't ask me to sugarcoat it."

"You're right, Jameson," Creighton acknowledged. "A man who can bring himself to do that to one human being won't hesitate to do it to another."

Marjorie sighed. "I wasn't protecting Michael Barnwell, I was protecting his family. But I suppose we're beyond that now."

"Who's Michael Barnwell?" Jameson asked.

Marjorie and Creighton described the meeting with Michael's wife, Elizabeth, and the trail of clues that led them to the house.

"Why didn't Mrs. Barnwell call the police?" the detective quizzed.

"Why didn't Mrs. Barnwell call the police?" Marjorie mimicked. "She did call the police, but they dismissed it as a domestic dispute."

"Well you should have called us the minute she showed up on your doorstep," he chided.

"Yes," Creighton interjected, "because we all know how quickly you act upon Marjorie's intuition."

"Careful," Jameson warned. "There's no need for this to get personal. I'm just saying that you could have called us before you started traipsing around a crime scene, destroying potential evidence."

"Yeah," Noonan interjected, "what gives with the bathroom? There's about two inches of water on the floor."

"Oh, that?" Marjorie replied as innocently as she could. "That's um … um … "

"Detective!" At once, a uniformed policeman appeared carrying a soaking wet navy blue dress shoe with what resembled a pair of giant tweezers. "Detective, we found what was causing the flood in the bathroom."

Jameson took the tweezers from the young man. "Hmmm. Why would someone try to flush a shoe? If it's a clue, why not burn it? Unless they wanted us to find it … "

"Excuse me," Marjorie pardoned herself as she surreptitiously grabbed the shoe.

"What are you doing? That's evidence!"

"No, I'm afraid it isn't. It's mine."

"Yours? How did your shoe get in the—?"

“The same way lemon drops adhere to dogs’ hindquarters and Model Ts appear in rearview mirrors every time she’s around,” Creighton explained. “I call it The Magic of Marjorie.”

“I call it screwy,” Noonan opined.

“I call it a waste of four dollars,” Marjorie said with disgust. “I loved these shoes!”

Jameson held up both hands as if directing traffic. “I don’t care what any of you call it. I want to get to the bottom of this.”

Creighton smirked. “If you found Marjorie’s shoe, you already have.”

Jameson huffed impatiently.

“Pardon the pun, but I’m quite serious. If Marjorie’s shoe hadn’t gotten flushed, we might never have gone down to the cellar. I was looking for the main shutoff valve for the plumbing when we discovered that the key that was in Michael Barnwell’s pocket opened the lock on the basement doors.”

“And inside?” the detective probed. “Did you happen to find anything inside the house that I should know about? After all, you two aren’t above pocketing evidence.”

Marjorie was indignant. “We didn’t ‘pocket’ anything. There was nothing to pocket—not a clue to be found. Oh, except the suitcase.”

“Suitcase?”

“Yes, the set by the back door. There’s a suitcase missing.”

“How do you know it’s missing?”

“Because I saw a similar set at Fox’s Department Store. They come in a set of four. If you look at Veronica Carter’s set, there’s only three.”

Noonan shrugged. “So? Veronica Carter packed her suitcase and left with Michael Barnwell.”

"There's two problems with that theory," Marjorie stated. "First, Veronica's neighbor, Mrs. Sullivan, claims that the last time she heard Veronica, she and another person—allegedly Michael—were having a terrible argument. Hardly the sort of testimony that makes one believe that they suddenly ran off together."

"Veronica might have changed her mind," Creighton offered. "Heaven knows, she wouldn't be the first woman to be fickle about a chap."

Jameson glanced at Marjorie and struggled to look elsewhere.

"Oops." Creighton realized too late what he had said. "Sorry, Jameson. No harm meant."

Marjorie blushed awkwardly before furthering her hypothesis. "You're right, Creighton, but Mrs. Sullivan's story makes it sound as though the confrontation was violent. She described yelling, screaming, and then—all of a sudden—silence. Veronica Carter is tough, worldly—I find it hard to believe she'd take off with a man who beat her."

"True enough," Creighton conceded. "What's the second problem?"

"Isn't it obvious? If Veronica Carter and Michael Barnwell ran off together, whose body is in the cellar?"

There was a long pause during which Noonan scratched his head. "Could you say that again?"

Marjorie ignored him.

"There's only one person who can tell us what happened here." Jameson's voice boomed, "We need to find Michael Barnwell!"

SIX

"PARDON ME?" MARJORIE FEIGNED deafness. "Did you just say that we need to find Barnwell?

Jameson nodded. "Uh-huh."

"I thought so. Perhaps it's my imagination, but that's exactly what Creighton and I were doing when this whole thing started." She addressed her fiancé. "Wasn't it, honey?"

"It certainly was," Creighton replied with a smug smile.

"Then we stumbled upon a body and, before we knew it, you and Noonan were on the scene. Not that it isn't nice seeing you again, Noonan," she added aside.

"Thanks. It's nice seeing you too," he answered in kind.

"Thank you," she stated gratefully. "And suddenly," she directed at Jameson, "you're barking orders, questioning us like common criminals, and acting as if you're the brains of this operation."

"Then what do you suggest?" Jameson asked.

Marjorie's eyes sparkled. "I suggest we split up and see who solves this mystery first."

"Yeah!" Creighton shouted, then thought twice. He looked at Marjorie questioningly. "Yeah?"

"Yeah," she affirmed. "Darling, when we found the body, you suggested that we would be able to wrap up the case by the end of the week."

"I did? Why... yes, I did... didn't I... darling?" Creighton laughed nervously. "In all the excitement, I had forgotten about that," he explained to a doubtful Jameson and Noonan.

"Yes, you did," she confirmed. "So what do you gentlemen say? Are we 'on'?"

Creighton grinned like a high school boy who had been promised a date to the prom. "Come now, Jameson, how can you refuse? It's the modern equivalent of a duel, old boy. First one who comes up with the suspect wins."

Marjorie had never before seen anyone lose all his or her natural color, but she could have sworn that Jameson turned gray at the suggestion of a challenge. Whatever he may have been feeling, however, he accepted—with gusto. "You're on!" He extended his hand to his female contestant.

She gleefully accepted, shaking Jameson's hand with vigor. "Loser accepts his lot gracefully and promises to view the winner as an equal."

"I think you mean 'equals' darling," Creighton reminded her.

"Sorry! Yes, loser accepts his lot gracefully and promises to view the 'winners' as equals."

Jameson relinquished Marjorie's hand with a nod and took Creighton's hand into his own. "Deal," he pronounced.

"Can I trade places with Creighton?" Noonan requested.

"No, you can't trade places with Creighton," Jameson snapped. "We're a team. We're invincible. We'll win this silly bet." He patted Noonan on the back—a gesture Marjorie and Creighton had never before witnessed.

Noonan looked at Marjorie pleadingly.

The writer laughed. "Why Noonan, you don't seem very confident. Could it be you don't think you're going to win?"

"Miss McClelland, my wife has taught me never to underestimate the female gender. I'd be dead ten times over if it weren't for her kindness and strength. She delivered two fine Noonan children without any help at all and still managed to put up with my nonsense. And as for you, well, you're screwy, but there must be something to all that screwiness, 'cause you've solved two cases out of two already."

Marjorie raised an eyebrow. "I'm sure there's a compliment hidden in there somewhere, but I can't quite put my finger on it."

"With all due respect to your kind, yet poorly worded tribute to Marjorie's talents," Creighton explained, "it's not you we're challenging, Noonan." His eyes shifted toward Jameson.

"You're challenging me?" the detective exclaimed.

"Why not? You challenge Marjorie and me any time we step into your world of crime. And, I must say, Marjorie's right on par with your skills."

"On par?" Jameson skeptically questioned. "I'm a trained professional."

"Well, I must call things as they are," Creighton replied. "Marjorie has a bold approach to investigative work, an eye for fitting clues together, and an unquenchable thirst for the truth."

"I have those things," Jameson averred.

"Perhaps, but there's one thing Marjorie has that you don't—"

"Just one thing?" Noonan interrupted.

"Keen intuition," Creighton completed the sentence.

"Intuition?" Jameson replied. "Detective work should be based upon cold, hard evidence, not conjecture."

"Ah, but how do you find that evidence unless you follow your hunches? Marjorie has an uncanny knack for sensing things that might slip by the rest of us. Why, as we approached this house, Marjorie could sense that something was wrong. She couldn't pinpoint what it was exactly, but she knew that things weren't as they should be. Unfortunately, she also has an uncanny ability to get herself into all manner of bizarre and embarrassing situations—such as getting her foot caught in a commode—but that should have no bearing whatsoever on her reputation as a detective, which, in my opinion, is excellent."

"Thank you," Marjorie replied. "I think."

"That's all nonsense," Jameson dismissed with a wave of his hand. "I admit Marjorie has had a hand in helping us solve a couple of cases, but her contributions were due to luck, not some female intuition gobbledygook."

"Luck you say? We'll see about that." Creighton offered his hand. "Until then, let the best team win."

Jameson accepted and the two men shook hands. Meanwhile, Noonan could be heard talking to himself in low plaintive tones: "I've gotta get a different partner …"

SEVEN

THE THIN, GRAY-HAIRED FIGURE of Dr. Joseph Heller climbed the cellar stairs somberly. "It's times like this I wish I were a dentist."

"Pretty bad, huh, Doc?" Noonan observed.

"That it is." The doctor shook his head. "Long as I live I'll never understand the things people do to each other."

"Any idea as to the cause of death?" Jameson queried.

"Can't say for certain, you understand," Heller responded with more than a hint of New England guardedness. "I have to take some tests yet, but my first guess would be loss of blood. Mind you that's just a guess at this point."

Jameson nodded. "Loss of blood from the severed limbs."

"From the severed limbs? No. The loss of her hands and feet had nothing to do with it—mind you, again, this is all hypothetical until I get back to the lab—but I'd say it was the beating that did her in. Internal bleeding."

Jameson was incredulous. "You're joking. I'd have thought the, um, 'amputations' would have caused more blood loss than the beating."

"Oh, they would have," Dr. Heller replied matter-of-factly as he removed his spectacles and placed them into the breast pocket of his brown suit jacket, "had she been alive when they occurred."

"What? You mean ... ?"

Heller nodded. "The hands and feet were cut off after she was dead."

"After," the detective repeated in disbelief.

"Let me get this straight," Noonan cut in. "Someone beat this girl to death and then ..."

"Got himself a saw," Heller confirmed.

Noonan's normally ruddy complexion turned a faint shade of green. "What kinda nutcase would do such a thing? It wasn't enough he bashed her face in, he had to hack her up too."

"Probably didn't want the body to be identified," Jameson surmised.

Heller's brow furrowed. "With all due respect, Detective, that doesn't quite fit with what I see here."

"What do you see here?"

"Well this is all off the record, of course."

"Yes, Joe. Yes, I know it's all off the record," Jameson exclaimed impatiently. "Just tell me what you see."

"Well, let's assume for a minute that you're the murderer trying to hide the identity of the victim. You'd make her face unrecognizable, naturally. And then you'd remove any chance of fingerprints being traced, correct?"

"If I thought the victim had fingerprints on file somewhere, yes."

"Mmm," Heller grunted in agreement. "How long would you wait to do it?"

"Huh?" Jameson and Noonan replied in unison.

"How long after the murder would you wait to remove the fingerprints or, in this case, hands?"

"I wouldn't wait," Jameson answered. "I'd do it right away."

"Exactly, but waiting is exactly what this fellow did. There's no sign of any bleeding from those wounds, meaning he waited for the blood of the victim to coagulate before going about his job. What's more, some of those cuts seem fresher than others."

"Care to explain what that means?" Jameson prodded.

"In English," Noonan added.

"It means that the murderer cut off a hand one day, a foot the next, and so forth."

"Jeez," Noonan remarked with disgust.

"Now you see why I don't think identity was the motive here." Heller frowned. "No, gentlemen, if you ask me, either this guy enjoyed what he was doing, or his plan was to dispose of the body—one piece at a time."

EIGHT

MARJORIE RAN TO HER bedroom closet and started pulling dresses from their hangers. "Oh no, not that," she muttered to herself before tossing the dress aside. "Oh, that has a small spot on the collar." Another garment went sailing onto the bedroom floor.

Creighton stood in her bedroom doorway. "Darling, Mrs. Patterson loves you regardless of what you're wearing."

"Mrs. Patterson? I was changing so that we could continue our investigation." Marjorie pulled off her stockings and rummaged through a dresser drawer for a fresh pair.

"Darling," Creighton stepped forward and grasped his fiancée by the shoulders. "We promised Mrs. Patterson we'd have dinner with her tonight. I've been looking forward to it. You've been looking forward to it."

"Yes, but that was before—" she bit her lip. "Oh Creighton, how can anyone do that to another human being? It's—it's—"

He took her into his arms and pulled her close. "I know, Marjorie. I really do, but there's nothing we can do tonight. It's almost five o'clock, a rainstorm is looming, and it's the perfect time for us to enjoy life and love, especially a certain someone who loves us—you—more than anything. Let's enjoy it while we can, darling."

Marjorie's body convulsed in sobs. "I just—I just . . . oh God, Creighton . . ."

"I know, darling. I know. I find it hard to put it out of my mind too. But we need to set those thoughts to rest for a little while, and who's better at comforting troubled souls than good ol' Mrs. Patterson?" He kissed her on the forehead. "Or maybe we should call her 'Mum'?"

Marjorie chuckled despite her tears. "She has been a mother to us both, hasn't she, Creighton?"

"Yes she has, darling. And she's exactly what we need."

Marjorie sat at Mrs. Patterson's porcelain-topped kitchen table, sipping a small glass of sherry.

Outdoors, a thunderstorm raged with a ferocity the likes of which Marjorie had never before seen. Given the day's events, Marjorie might have viewed the storm as a warning of future misfortune, but here, with Mrs. Patterson, Creighton, and her cat, Sam, she felt at ease for the first time all day.

Emily Patterson, a small, birdlike woman of approximately seventy years of age, lived diagonally across the street from the McClelland home, but the relationship between the two women ran far deeper than that of good neighbors. Indeed, it seemed some divine stroke of providence that Marjorie, abandoned as an infant by a mother who sought a career on the stage, and Emily Patterson, a woman who had longed for children but could have none of her own, should reside just a few yards from each other.

The past twenty-seven years had seen the deaths of both Marjorie's father and Mrs. Patterson's husband, yet the two women survived and grew even closer, their shared grief only strengthening the bond of loss that had initially brought them together.

Mrs. Patterson appeared at Marjorie's side and, with trembling hands, placed a platter of roast chicken in the center of the table. "You poor dears!" she exclaimed. "Going all day without a thing to eat. It's not healthy, you know."

Creighton and Marjorie exchanged complacent grins while Sam curled up on his mistress's lap.

"Now then, there's mashed potatoes, fresh peas, and home-baked bread, so eat up, you two."

Marjorie rose from her position, Sam in her arms. "Thank you, Mrs. Patterson." She kissed the elderly woman on the cheek.

"Yes, thanks, Mrs. P." Creighton kissed the other side of Mrs. Patterson's face.

Her blue eyes filled with tears. "Oh, stop it now," she pooh-poohed. "You know how I feel about you kids."

Creighton assisted Mrs. Patterson into her chair. "Yes, but that doesn't mean we shouldn't show some appreciation and, God forbid, even help you from time to time."

"You mean 'try' to help her," Marjorie corrected. "She's too stubborn to accept help from anyone."

"That's not true," Emily Patterson averred. "I could use your help now in eating this dinner."

"No one can say you ask for too much, Mrs. P.," Creighton replied as he placed a meaty drumstick on his plate.

Mrs. Patterson blushed and giggled like a woman one-third her age. "Well now, tell me, what did you two do today?"

Marjorie glanced across the table at her fiancé.

Creighton fixed his eyes on his dinner and pretended to be fascinated by the process of rearranging peas on his plate.

"Um," Marjorie stalled. "Umm, we got involved in a missing person's case."

"A what?"

"A missing person's case," she reiterated before taking another sip of sherry. Creighton, meanwhile, quietly ate his dinner.

"Sleuthing? I thought you were going to work on your book this morning and then discuss your wedding plans this afternoon."

"Y-yes, but—"

"But what?"

"But that was before this woman showed up on my doorstep. She's young—nineteen if she's a day—and has a baby, a boy. Her husband's been missing for three days now, and I . . . well, I couldn't turn her away."

"Why did she go to you? Why not the police?" Mrs. Patterson asked, trying to remain coolly detached and disapproving despite her growing curiosity.

"She did go to the police," Creighton answered in between chews. "They gave her the typical hysterical-female treatment. Then she remembered Marjorie's name from the papers and decided to look her up."

Mrs. Patterson cut into a slice of breast meat and sighed. "Poor dear. I can understand why you wanted to help her, but you know you do need to make some time for yourselves. Now that all of Connecticut knows that you're amateur detectives, you're going to have all sorts of people knocking on your door. I know it sounds terrible, but you can't help all of them—there simply isn't enough time in the day, and right now the two of you need to get on with your lives."

"But—" Marjorie started.

"No 'buts.' You can help that girl find her husband by calling Detective Jameson and asking him to look into it. I'm sure he'd be glad to do it, and his involvement would free you up to go forward with your wedding plans."

Marjorie buttered a slice of bread and glanced sheepishly at Creighton, who returned the guilty look with one of his own. "That's a bang-up idea, Mrs. Patterson," he stated, "except that—that . . . well . . . he already knows."

"Wonderful," Mrs. Patterson declared as she dug into her mashed potatoes. "Now that that's settled, perhaps, Marjorie, if you're not too busy this week, we can look over some wedding dress patterns. And Creighton, I told you that the church league and I would be more than happy to provide for the reception."

"Yes, the church league," Creighton said slowly.

"I know it's probably not as fancy as the weddings you're used to attending, Creighton, but it's the way we small-town people do things. When a couple plans a wedding, they get married in church and then go to the parish hall for sandwiches, punch, and cake. All the women in the community pitch in by bringing something. I'm going to make my salmon tea sandwiches, and I found a recipe in *Good Housekeeping* magazine for a white cake with divinity frosting, which would make a wonderful wedding cake."

"Oh, I um," Marjorie was reluctant to hurt Mrs. Patterson's feelings, but she had to tell the truth, "I already spoke with Creighton's cook regarding the cake. She wanted to do it, and I do love her baking. Not that I don't love yours, of course!"

"Don't be silly! I know you do." Mrs. Patterson sat back in her chair and grabbed Marjorie and Creighton's hands. "I'm sorry. I'm afraid I'm getting as bossy as Louise Schutt. It's just that I'm so excited and happy for you both!"

"You have no reason to apologize, Mrs. Patterson," Marjorie said while squeezing the elderly woman's hand. "We're excited too. We're just not sure what kind of wedding we want yet. But, if we can get enough time, we'll try to arrange everything this week. I can't make any promises because we have some things to … to …"

"Wrap up?" Creighton offered with a grin.

"Yes, wrap up," she shot him a snotty look. "But I'm sure we can work something in. And whatever won't fit this week, we can do the week after."

Creighton nodded. "God willing," he added sotto voce.

"Good!" Mrs. Patterson giggled excitedly and raised her glass of iced tea. "To making a perfect wedding."

Marjorie and Creighton clinked their glasses. "To making a perfect wedding," they repeated before taking a sip of their beverages. As they drank, their eyes met and it was apparent that they shared the same thought.

Creighton leaned against the fireplace mantle in the study of Kensington House, the Georgian mansion he had purchased just a few months earlier. Since then, he had done much to make it into a beautiful, yet cozy, living space, replete with classic charm as well as the most modern amenities.

"So now, not only do we need to solve this case before Jameson does, but we need to simultaneously arrange for a church ceremony, plan a reception menu, and you have to select a wedding gown? Throw a book deadline into that mix, and you'll have the makings of a complete nervous breakdown." He swirled a fair amount of brandy in a crystal snifter. "I don't know why you didn't just tell Mrs. Patterson about the murder. It would have bought us more time."

Marjorie was ensconced in a high-back wing chair, enjoying the warmth of the fire. Since the rain, the evening had turned quite cool and breezy—a portent of the autumn days soon to come. She swirled her brandy pensively. "I didn't want to hear her lecture me about how I think too much about death and not enough about life. You heard the way she carried on about the missing person's case. Could you imagine if we had told her the truth?" She sighed. "Besides, she's so excited about our wedding."

"I am too, darling, but let's not forget that it is exactly that: our wedding. No one else's." He knelt before her and kissed her passionately. "I'm anxious to call you my wife, but I don't want to get ourselves stuck in a wedding that meets everyone else's expectations but yours. I want you to be happy—I'm sure you've dreamed of it since you were a little girl. As for me, I'd be satisfied with any ceremony that made you Mrs. Ashcroft. But what about you, darling? What do you want for a wedding? What's your idea of perfection?"

"I don't know. I used to think that it was a church wedding with lots of flowers and the entire town in attendance, but now—now, I just don't know." She sighed and took a sip of brandy. "Although maybe this isn't the right time. By tomorrow morning I'll be my chipper old self, dreaming of orange blossoms and white chiffon. But for now…"

Creighton nodded. "I'm having trouble forgetting it too." He rose from his knees and plopped into the wing chair opposite his fiancée. A few minutes transpired before he spoke again: "Stay here tonight, Marjorie."

The young woman's eyes grew wide.

"No," Creighton clarified. "I don't mean it that way. Just stay here so that—well, life is very short isn't it? Fragile even. One moment alive and well, the next moment lying in a dank cellar or God knows where else." He blinked back the tears in his eyes. "Stay here tonight, Marjorie, so I can look after you and know that you're safe."

Marjorie laughed softly. She understood the fear Creighton harbored, for the loss of his mother was still as real to Creighton as the loss of Marjorie's father was to her. "Creighton, darling," she reassured him. "Of course I'm safe. Nothing's going to happen to me."

He rose from his seat and knelt before her once again. "I know you're safe—at least my brain does, but my heart—"

Marjorie placed a delicate finger to his lips. "Your heart needn't doubt a thing." With that, she kissed him passionately, and Creighton Ashcroft wondered if he weren't the luckiest man on earth.

NINE

Creighton awoke the next morning to the sound of Marjorie's laughter resonating from the pool area and wafting, with the cool summer breeze, through his open bedroom windows.

He donned his bathrobe and slippers and shuffled downstairs. The late August morning was resplendent with the aroma of honeysuckle as the sun shone bright upon Marjorie's golden head.

Both Agnes, Creighton's cook, and Arthur, Creighton's butler, were seated at the pale-green aluminum patio set, paying rapt attention to Marjorie's animated tale of a Catholic priest who had drunk too much wine. "So the redheaded priest says, 'Mrs. Kilkenny, I don't know who the father of your children is, but—'"

At the sight of her intended groom, she stopped mid-sentence, causing Agnes and Arthur to leap to attention.

Without a word, Creighton lifted a chestnut-colored eyebrow in his fiancée's direction.

Marjorie mimicked the gesture and grinned broadly. "Don't go running off now," she told Agnes and Arthur. "Not that the joke's very funny, but it's not that bad either. Isn't that right, Mr. Ashcroft?"

Creighton beamed and stepped forward to take the spot beside his future bride. "Oh, I don't know. I think it's one of your best."

Agnes and Arthur breathed a sigh of relief, glanced at each other, and took their seats.

The pair stood up fifteen minutes later despite their raucous laughter.

"Oh madam, I should check on those cinnamon rolls, I know they're your favorite." She took Marjorie by the hand. "I'm so looking forward to making your wedding cake and having you as mistress of Kensington House," she announced before scurrying into the kitchen.

Arthur glanced awkwardly at his watch. "High time we received the *Wall Street Journal*, don't you think, sir? I'd best go check." He stood up, clicked the heels of his highly polished black dress shoes, and made his way into the house, but not before a parting comment to Marjorie. "It is very good to have you here, miss. Why, you act on all of us like a tonic—especially Mr. Ashcroft."

Marjorie blushed. "I could get used to mornings like this. How about you?"

Creighton smiled. "Yes, I could. I could get used to nights like last night too."

She gasped dramatically. "Mr. Ashcroft, how dare—"

"Oh, I won't say another word. How could I? However, I might ask you what's on our agenda for today."

"I've been thinking about that. I believe we should check on where Michael Barnwell worked."

"Where's that?" Creighton asked as he propped his feet upon an adjacent chair and drank his black coffee.

"An insurance company, but I'm not sure which one. We may need to call Elizabeth Barnwell." Marjorie poured herself another cup of coffee and added one teaspoon of sugar and a few drops of cream.

"Are you going to tell her about the body?"

"No. I think we need to investigate a bit further before we break that kind of news. Besides, all we have linking Michael to the house is a scrap of paper, a key, and the testimony of a nosy neighbor who claims she saw a man with a mustache. Do you know how many men have mustaches?"

"In this country or the world?"

Marjorie narrowed her eyes.

"Sorry," Creighton excused. "That was a rhetorical question, wasn't it?"

"As I was saying," Marjorie continued, "Elizabeth and little Michael have been through enough. I'd prefer to spare them any further upset until we have all the facts. In the meantime, we'll call her and say that we have a few leads, but that we'd like to check his office since he spent so much time there."

"'We'll' call Elizabeth Barnwell?"

"What?" Marjorie answered blankly.

"You said 'we' but I'm certain that you mean 'me.'"

Marjorie sipped her coffee innocently as Agnes placed a basket of warm cinnamon buns beside her. "I'm certain I did too." Her green eyes sparkled.

After a brief call to Elizabeth Barnwell, Marjorie and Creighton traveled to the New England Allied Insurance Company to speak with Michael's employer, Benjamin Sachs. What Mr. Sachs might be able to tell them, they did not know, but if Elizabeth's timeline was correct, he may have been the last person to see Michael before his disappearance.

A tweed-clad secretary emerged from behind a frosted glass door. "Mr. Sachs will see you now."

Marjorie and Creighton shuffled into the tiny wood-paneled room. Benjamin Sachs was a small, balding man whose slender physique seemed to float in the bagginess of his poorly tailored suit. He rose to his feet, removed the cigar from his mouth with one hand, and reached across the shabby desk with the other. "Benjamin Sachs. And you are?"

Creighton shook the man's hand vigorously. "Creighton Ashcroft. And this is my fiancée, Miss Marjorie McClelland."

Sachs smiled at the young writer. "Pleased to make your acquaintance. Sit down." He gestured to a small, upholstered seat. "I'll have my secretary bring in an extra chair."

"That won't be necessary," Creighton assured. "I'm fine."

"Suit yourself," Sachs replied before sitting down again. "So, how can I help you?"

"We need to speak to you about an employee of yours—Michael Barnwell," Marjorie announced.

"Barnwell?" Sachs placed the cigar between his lips and took a few nervous puffs. "What do you need to know about him?"

"His wife reported him missing. We need to know the last time you saw him." Marjorie conveniently omitted anything to do with Veronica Carter and the body they had found in the cellar.

"Saw him? Saw him ... saw him ..." he repeated as if it were a magical incantation. He suddenly snapped his fingers. "Why, that would have been the day before yesterday. Came in here, jittery as can be. Mind you, Barnwell's always wound pretty tight, but that day, he was a bundle of nerves. Didn't even blink when I was talking to him."

"Did he say what was bothering him?" Creighton ventured.

"Bothering him? Bothering him ... bothering him ... no. He asked for some time off, which I gave him, but he didn't say anything else. Not that he would. He never talked much about his personal life. Policies, however," he snapped his fingers again, "that was a different story altogether. He could talk for hours—and I do mean hours—about how adding certain clauses to our policies might benefit the company. Yes, sir, he was an Allied man all right."

"An allied man?" Marjorie said again.

"Why, Allied Insurance Company, of course." He smiled.

She politely returned the smile. "Of course."

"So I suppose it's safe to assume that Michael is a good employee?" Creighton ventured.

"Good? He's the best claims adjustor we have—saved us thousands of dollars in false claims since he started here three years ago."

"I'm sure that's earned him a lot of friends," Creighton commented facetiously.

"It has here at Allied," Sachs affirmed. "Not that it makes a cent of difference to Barnwell. He keeps to himself. A real loner."

"And you're certain, Mr. Sachs, that you last saw Michael Barnwell two days ago?" Marjorie quizzed.

Sachs eyed the calendar on the wall. "Let's see, today's Thursday... yes, it was Tuesday I saw him. I remember because my wife had just phoned to ask me to pick up a few things from the store on the way home from work—my mother-in-law was arriving that night for a week-long visit. I don't get along well with my mother-in-law," he added delicately, "so I was in a bit of a huff when I hung up and decided to go to lunch. That's when I literally bumped into Barnwell. He was coming in as I was going out."

"Where had he gone?"

"I don't know. I didn't ask. When a claims adjustor makes as much money for the company as Michael Barnwell does, you tend to turn a blind eye to the finer details."

Creighton nodded. "However, you did notice that he was extremely nervous. Didn't that strike you as somewhat odd?"

Sachs tossed his head back and forth in contemplation. "Yes and no. As I said earlier, Barnwell has always been on the edgy side. Was he edgier than usual? Sure, but he'd also been working on an important claim. Big money at stake—for both sides."

"Interesting. What type of claim was it?" Marjorie asked casually.

"A life insurance claim. I'm not at liberty to say anything else, however."

"We understand," Creighton acknowledged.

"Oh, of course," Marjorie interjected. "We would never dream of compromising your client's privacy. We're just doing everything we can to find Michael and bring him back to his wife and child. I don't suppose... no, I shouldn't even ask. You've done so much already."

Sachs learned forward and patted Marjorie's hand, which rested upon the surface of the desk. "No, no, please. Anything I can do to help."

Creighton laughed inwardly at the ease with which his fiancée could ply her feminine wiles. Yet he couldn't help but wish that she'd take more effort in displaying her engagement ring.

"Well," she started, "we'd like to take a look at his desk. Just to see if he left behind any clues that might indicate his whereabouts. But I don't wish to impose..." Creighton could have sworn that she punctuated the sentence with a flutter of her eyelashes.

Sachs rose from his chair and walked to the other side of the desk where he, again, took Marjorie's hand in his. "Don't be silly, dear. Of course you can see his desk. It's not as if you're asking to rummage through our file cabinets."

Marjorie flashed Creighton a triumphant grin as Sachs led them out of his office and into the turbulence of the New England Allied Insurance hurricane. The cacophony of ringing telephones, tapping typewriters, and monotonous secretaries' voices filled the stale air of the vast, windowless room where neatly attired agents crunched numbers at row-upon-row of evenly spaced wooden desks.

A tired-looking young man approached Sachs. "Sir! Sir? My cousin just graduated from college in May, and I was wondering if—?"

"Tell him to come in and fill out an application," the older man answered abruptly.

"Oh thank you, sir. He'll be very happy. He's a great..." His voiced faded into the office din as Sachs walked away, leading Marjorie and Creighton farther into the sea of clerks, secretaries, and eager-to-please new agents.

Marjorie frowned. She had never underestimated the effects of the economic depression; she knew she was quite fortunate to have what she did. But when America's best and brightest were competing to work in a soulless environment such as this, hopes of recovery seemed to dissipate as quickly as the graduates' youthful dreams.

Sachs pointed to the far left corner of the room. "That's Barnwell's desk right there."

The desk surface was empty except for a telephone, the edges of which were aligned perfectly with the corner of the desk, and four pencils arranged, neatly, in a row.

"As you can see," Sachs continued, "there's nothing to see."

Creighton walked behind the desk. "Well, I guess that's it," he declared as he flopped into the revolving wooden chair. He leaned back and crossed his legs. As he did so, the toe of his shoe struck something with a loud thud. "Hullo . . . ?"

"What is it?" Marjorie asked.

Creighton peered beneath the desk. "It's a box of some kind." He bent down and retrieved the item, which was marked with the familiar initials *V.C.*

"The missing suitcase!" Marjorie gasped.

Creighton placed it on the desk and, with a quick motion, sprung open the lid. The case was empty, but the lining was stained with a reddish-brown substance.

"Good lord!" Sachs exclaimed. "Is that what I think it is?"

Creighton slid an arm around Marjorie's waist and tipped his hat upward. "It certainly isn't Bosco."

TEN

Creighton and Marjorie were sipping coffee from earthenware mugs when Detective Jameson strutted into Dr. Heller's lab, followed closely by Officer Noonan.

"I got your phone call," Jameson cracked. "What's the matter? Giving up on the case?"

"No, we're not giving up. And, 'we' didn't call you," Marjorie clarified. "The officer who took our call did."

"Your call? Don't tell me you found another dead body."

"They're corpses, Jameson," Creighton countered, "not rabbits."

"Before you start mocking our efforts, what, precisely, were you doing all day?" Marjorie questioned.

"Looking into Veronica Carter's background," Jameson rebutted. "One of the first rules of detective work is the better you get to know your victim, the better the chance you'll find the motive. Once you find the motive, you find the murderer."

"*School-Age Sleuth Magazine*, May 9, 1932," Creighton whispered in Marjorie's ear.

Marjorie suppressed a giggle as Jameson continued his lecture on modern detective work. "Veronica Carter was the classic victim of this sort of crime: young, female, lower class, promiscuous. Tell them what we found, Noonan."

"Pretty average stuff," Noonan commented before reading from his pocket-sized notebook. "Ronnie Carter was twenty-two. Born and raised in Hartford. Dropped out of school at sixteen. Left home at seventeen. Worked as a waitress at seven different joints during the past five years. Latest job was at the Five O'Clock Diner in downtown Hartford. When Ronnie didn't show up for work three days ago, another waitress there got worried. She called Ronnie's friend and former roommate, Diana Hoffman. Hoffman had no idea where Ronnie was, but wasn't worried. Said that it was a habit of Ronnie's to pick up and leave without warning—especially when a guy was involved."

"Sounds like you know your victim," Marjorie noted. "So, what was the killer's motive?"

Jameson cleared his throat. "We haven't figured that out yet. But, mark my words, we will."

Dr. Heller breezed through the doors of the adjoining room. "Detective. Officer," he addressed. "I'm glad you're here. Miss McClelland and Mr. Ashcroft have uncovered a very valuable piece of evidence."

"What now?" Jameson grumbled.

"Oh, you'll like this one," Creighton prodded. "It may be our best piece of evidence yet."

"Can we hurry this up?" Jameson snarled.

"Of course," Heller replied as he lifted the sheet that concealed the piece of evidence in question.

"Veronica Carter's suitcase," Jameson stated in astonishment. "Where did you find this?"

"At the New England Allied Insurance Company," Marjorie answered. "Under Michael Barnwell's desk."

"What's more, the interior of the case is stained with blood," Creighton added.

"And I've found that the blood in the case is the same type as that of the victim," Heller announced.

"Looks like we may win that bet," Creighton asserted cockily.

"No one's winning any bet," Jameson corrected. "We may have evidence, but we still don't have a motive. Not for killing Veronica Carter, or for cutting off her hands and feet like he did."

"I might be able to shed some light there," Heller intervened. "The blood in the suitcase is consistent with the theory I had discussed with Detective Jameson and Officer Noonan. A theory my lab work has now substantiated."

"And that is?" Marjorie inquired.

"The hands and feet of the victim were severed and removed at different times—markedly different times. As if the killer removed a hand one day, a foot the next, and so forth. Apart from mental insanity, the only reason I could conceive of for a murderer to do such a thing is as a means of disposing the body."

The color drained from Marjorie's face. "Mrs. Sullivan said Veronica's latest boyfriend was always carrying a case. She had no idea what was in it…"

“Jeezus,” Noonan whispered as he mopped the perspiration from his green-tinged brow. “You mean he was carrying her out in pieces? In her own suitcase?”

“I’m not a detective, but it does fit with the evidence,” Heller explained.

Jameson removed his hat and ran a hand through his thick, dark brown hair. “We still don’t have a motive.”

“I can probably help with that one too,” Heller offered. “During the autopsy, I made a startling discovery. Veronica Carter was two and a half months pregnant.”

“That’s a motive all right,” Creighton commented. “Especially if Veronica threatened to tell Elizabeth.”

“Or expected Michael to divorce Elizabeth and marry her,” Marjorie continued.

“Noonan,” Jameson shouted, even though the officer was standing nearby. “Put an APB out on Michael Barnwell. I’m going to talk to his wife.”

“You’re not going to tell her about the body and the suitcase are you?” Marjorie asked.

“Of course I am. I have to. Her husband is the prime suspect in a murder investigation. We need to find him and bring him in.”

“But she doesn’t know where Michael is. That’s why she came to me.”

“Then she has nothing to worry about, does she?”

“Wait a minute,” she exclaimed as she grabbed her gloves, hat, and handbag. “Creighton and I are going with you. Elizabeth Barnwell is my client—”

“Our client, darling,” Creighton reminded.

"Our client," Marjorie amended. "We should be the ones to break the news. Besides, you're um ... well, let's just say it would go over better coming from someone with a gentle touch."

"That's a heck of a thing coming from Miss Hit-and-Run! 'Oh Robert, I don't think we should get married,'" Jameson mimicked. "I'll have you know I'm quite capable of breaking news gently. A lot better than someone else I know."

"Care to put your money where your mouth is?" Marjorie dared.

"Do you?" Jameson matched.

"Please! No more bets!" Creighton shouted in exasperation as he swung open the door to the lab. "Good Lord, what's wrong with you two?"

ELEVEN

The Barnwell residence was a tidy brick home on the outskirts of Ridgebury. Neatly trimmed hedges surrounded the postage-stamp-sized property, and the lawn, although slightly brown from the drying effects of the summer sun, was manicured to a horticultural perfection.

Marjorie stepped onto the brick front stoop and tapped lightly on the wood-framed storm door.

Elizabeth appeared almost instantly. "Oh, Miss McClelland! I'm so glad it's you. I was putting little Michael down for a nap when I saw the police car pull into the driveway. It's not Michael is it? He's not… dead… is he?"

"No, Mrs. Barnwell, it's nothing like that." Jameson flashed his badge. "Hartford County Police. May we come inside?"

Elizabeth glanced about nervously. "I-I-I guess so." She nudged the door open tentatively, allowing the trio admittance.

The dichotomy between the interior of the house and its exterior could not have been greater. Whereas outdoors neatness was the order of the day, indoors, madness reigned. Newspapers were strewn about the living room rug, dirty plates and glasses were scattered along the length of the coffee table, and a laundry basket, its contents neatly folded, yet so gray as to make one think that they were dirty, rather than freshly cleaned, occupied the overstuffed sofa.

Elizabeth stood by the room's only vacant chair and wrung her hands nervously. "I'm sorry I didn't get a chance to clean—it's been hard with Michael gone. The baby misses him so much, he's barely slept. I've been up with him most of the night."

"We understand," Marjorie assured.

"Have you found Michael?" Elizabeth asked hopefully.

"No, I'm afraid we haven't yet. But we're still looking."

"You haven't? But I need him! Little Michael needs him. You must find him. Soon!"

Marjorie eased the other woman gently into the chair. "We will find him. We just need to ask you a few questions to help us in our search. But you need to relax first. How about a glass of water?"

Elizabeth nodded. "Okay."

"I'll get it," Creighton offered and made his way into the adjacent kitchen. The area, like the living room, was in a state of disarray. The linoleum floor was littered with crumbs, and dirty dishes overflowed the kitchen sink.

Fearful of contracting some rare disease, Creighton decided against reaching into the sink and cleaning a glass. "Elizabeth," he called. "Where would I find the glasses?"

"Oh, um, they're in the cupboard above the sink."

Creighton opened the cupboard doors, but all that came into view was some flour, sugar, and some baking soda. "No, that's not it. Anywhere else I might find them?"

Elizabeth blushed. "Oh! Oh, I'm so sorry. I forgot I rearranged the kitchen shelves a few weeks ago."

"Don't worry," Marjorie smiled. "Creighton's very resourceful."

Creighton lived up to Marjorie's claims by returning with a teacup filled with cold water. He handed it to Elizabeth. "Here, drink this up."

Elizabeth did as instructed.

"Thank you. I do feel a little better now." She tucked a wisp of wayward brown hair behind one ear. "What did you want to ask me?"

Jameson stepped forward. "Do you know anyone by the name of Veronica Carter?"

"No. Why? What does she have to do with Michael?" She turned to Marjorie, her voice pleading. "Miss McClelland, what is he trying to say?"

Marjorie heaved a heavy sigh. "I'm sorry, Elizabeth. I truly am. But I don't know how else to tell you..."

"Other than to just say it," Jameson finished the sentence impatiently. "We have reason to believe that Veronica Carter was your husband's mistress."

Elizabeth leapt from her chair. "That can't be! Michael wouldn't do that to me! That woman is a liar!"

Creighton, Jameson, and Marjorie tried to calm her, but to no avail.

"Let go of me," she shouted as Creighton placed a hand on her shoulder. "Let go of me! I'm going to see this Veronica woman and give her a piece of my mind! Telling people that Michael—my Michael—"

She was cut short by the shrill scream of a young child.

"Oh! Michael, my baby! Mommy's sorry, sweetie." She ran to her son's bedroom and retrieved the bawling youngster. "Detective Jameson," she addressed over her son's wails, "I want you to tell Veronica Carter to stop spreading lies about my husband. You see for yourself what it's doing to my family."

"Mrs. Barnwell, we didn't speak with Veronica Carter," Jameson explained. "Veronica Carter is dead. She was murdered about the same time your husband disappeared."

Marjorie took little Michael from his mother's arms as Jameson continued.

"We also found a suitcase, stained with Veronica's blood, under your husband's desk at work. In short, we suspect your husband of murdering Veronica Carter."

"One minute you say he's having an affair. The next minute he's murdering the woman. It doesn't make any sense! Why would he do such a thing?"

"We can't be sure of motive until we speak with your husband, but we suspect it was because Veronica Carter was pregnant with his child."

"Pregnant? A baby? But, Michael Jr … he …" Elizabeth started to argue. Then, with a loud sigh, she promptly fainted.

While Marjorie placed a sleeping Michael Jr. back in his crib, Creighton and Jameson cleared the laundry from the sofa and lifted an unconscious Elizabeth Barnwell onto it.

"Nice job of breaking the news gently," Creighton quipped as he positioned a pillow beneath the woman's head. "It had all the grace of an Elliot Ness raid."

"Come on," Jameson protested. "I wasn't that hard on her." He looked to Marjorie, who had just reentered the living room, for validation. "Was I?"

"Let's just say the Mayo Clinic will never hire you to hand out diagnoses," the writer answered honestly.

Elizabeth Barnwell groaned.

"I know it wasn't the best joke, but I thought it was rather funny," Marjorie said defensively.

"No, darling," Creighton pointed to the woman on the sofa. "The groan came from her."

Elizabeth's eyes slowly opened as she emitted another soft groan. "What happened?"

"You fainted," Creighton informed her.

"And little Michael? Where is he?" she asked as she propped herself up on one elbow.

"Don't get up," Marjorie took her by the arm and eased her back into a reclining position. "The baby's fine. I put him back down for his nap."

Elizabeth relaxed and let her head sink back into the pillow. "Thank you. Thank you for taking care of him and me. I only wish there was something someone could do for Michael right now. I know he wouldn't do the terrible things you're saying. I just know it."

"There is a way for you to help him," Jameson offered. "Tell us where we can find him."

"I don't know," Elizabeth insisted. "And even if I did, I don't see how telling you would help him. You're only looking for him so that you can arrest him. When he didn't come home from work, I went to the police to report him missing. You know what happened? No one lifted a finger to help me. But now that you think he's committed a crime, you're doing everything you can to find him. You probably have every cop in Connecticut on the manhunt."

"Elizabeth," Marjorie urged. "I know you're upset and angry. I don't blame you. For the moment, however, we need to put that aside and all work together. If your husband is, indeed, innocent, then he must come forward and tell his side of the story. That way we—and the police—can look for the real killer."

Elizabeth mulled over Marjorie's words. "And what if Detective Jameson's right? What if you're all right? What if my husband was seeing this woman and I didn't know it? Worse yet, what if he did kill her?"

"Even more reason for him to come forward. If the police need to use force to bring him in, he could get hurt," Creighton reasoned.

Elizabeth buried her face in her hands and sobbed. After a few moments, she regained composure and, between sniffles, stated in an oddly composed voice: "Michael and I had some problems last year. Marital problems. He left for a while and went to his parents' house in Massachusetts. He might go there again."

"Did you try calling there?" Jameson asked.

Elizabeth replied in the negative. "They don't like me much. Even if Michael were there, I doubt they'd tell me."

Marjorie, Creighton, and Jameson exchanged hopeful glances. "Worth a shot, I suppose," Creighton deemed.

"Could you write down the address for us?" Jameson pulled a small pencil and a notepad from his jacket pocket.

Elizabeth took them and scrawled the house number and street name of an address in Springfield, Massachusetts. She handed the pad and the pencil back to Jameson and, once again, began to sob. "Oh Michael," she exclaimed between sharp intakes of air. "Oh Michael, forgive me."

TWELVE

SPRINGFIELD POLICE DETECTIVE THOMAS Butler was a tall, thin man with intensely blue eyes and an energetic disposition that bordered on edginess. "Hi Bob. I got my men over here as soon as I received your call. He was in the backyard smoking a cigarette when we arrived. Didn't see us though. Good thing he lives down the road from a drugstore," he pointed to the building behind him. "It's provided us with a good cover."

"Thanks, Tom," Jameson responded courteously. "You're sure he's still in there?" Jameson gestured toward the brick-faced building down the road.

"I'd bet my mother's soul on it—may she rest in peace." Butler blessed himself piously. "A couple of my guys are excellent shots. Would you like them to fix their guns on the windows and doors?"

Jameson cleared his throat and looked to his companions. "No, I don't think that will be necessary."

"You sure? I got a good look at him."

"Why? Is he a big guy? Does he look unstable?"

"No, nothing like that. I just know his type." Butler elaborated, "Seen it time and time before. Polite and neat-as-you-please on the surface, but underneath? Nothing but ice water and steel in his veins." His eye went to Marjorie. "But here now, a sweet little lady like you doesn't want to hear such things."

Marjorie shook her head. "On the contrary, I find them fascinating. I write about them all the time." She extended a hand, "Marjorie McClelland."

Butler took it in his own. "Ahhh, the mystery novelist?"

Marjorie nodded. "One and the same."

"The missus and I love your books. If there's nothing on the radio, she reads them aloud. Twenty years on the force and I haven't been able to solve one yet." He turned his attention to Creighton. "And who may this tall man be?"

Creighton shook the older detective's hand. "Creighton Ashcroft." He decided it best to leave off "the third."

"You're not actually engaged to this lovely creature, are you?" Butler waved a hand in Marjorie's direction.

"Yes, actually, I am."

"Some men have all the luck. Though I'm certain luck had nothing to do with it. You'd have to be pretty smart to have a girl like Miss McClelland even give you the time of day. I know, because Mrs. Butler is quite the clever cookie herself. I used to flatter myself that she married me because I was smarter than she was, but now I realize she married me because I wasn't as dumb as the other fellows she knew."

Marjorie and Creighton laughed.

"Anyways," Butler segued, "here we are carrying on like a bunch of hens at a tea party when there's a murderer to apprehend." He turned to Jameson. "How do you want to do this, Bob? Because I'll tell you right now, if you go in there flashing your badge, this guy could get violent."

Jameson bit his lip and remained silent.

"I've seen his type before, sir," Butler pressed. "He'll do anything to save himself. If he thinks we mean to put him away, he won't think twice about slitting your throat."

"I can't believe he's that dangerous," Marjorie averred. "His wife would certainly have seen that side of him by now, yet she's completely devoted to him. And what about his little boy?"

"Even cold-blooded killers have people who love them," Butler stated. "I've seen women stand by men who treated them and their children as punching bags. Why? Because they love them. Do they want things to be better? Sure. Are they ready to ditch the guy and get someone better? Not on your life." He frowned self-consciously. "Sorry, Miss McClelland. I didn't mean to carry on so."

"There's no reason to apologize. I'm sure you know a lot more than I do about criminal personalities. After all, you see a lot of them in your line of work," she replied. "However, I didn't get that impression about Michael and Elizabeth. Elizabeth was genuinely upset and concerned about her husband's disappearance. If he were as wicked as you say, I can't help but think she'd be happy to see him go."

Butler nodded solemnly. "Well, for the sake of his wife and child, I hope your intuition is stronger than mine. For the moment, however, I think we should treat this guy with kid gloves."

"I agree with Butler," Creighton opined. "Barnwell's boss called him an 'edgy' sort of fellow, even on a good day. Given the situation he's in, his nerves are doubtlessly worn thin by now. The sight of a Hartford County Police Detective beating down his front door could spur him to take drastic action. However, a private detective hired by his wife might be less provocative."

"A private detective?" the other three asked obtusely.

"Me," Creighton nearly screamed.

"Oh," Jameson and Butler sang in unison.

"But darling," Marjorie exclaimed. "What if Michael finds out that you're working with the police? You could be hurt... or worse!" She flung her arms around his neck and held him tightly. "Why, I think it's a stupid idea. Trying to apprehend a suspected murderer by yourself."

"Don't worry, sweetheart, I'll be fine." Creighton gave his fiancée a kiss on the forehead before gently pushing her away. "And, if not, that diamond on your finger will buy you more than a few chicken dinners."

"Or a nice inscription on your tombstone:

'Be it snatching lemon drops from dogs' behinds,
Or dressing in tuxes up to the nines,
Mr. Ashcroft viewed manners as a form of art.
If only his brain were as big as his heart.'"

"That's a lovely send-off, darling. I thought you only wrote mysteries, but here you are, Ridgebury's very own poet laureate." He raised an inquisitive eyebrow. "It seemed awfully polished, though... how long have you been working on that epitaph anyway?"

"Oh, go on and get killed." Marjorie scowled.

Creighton laughed and headed off down the road, whistling happily.

The elder Barnwell's house was a handsome red saltbox structure, which had been modified to accommodate two families.

Creighton pressed the buzzer labeled *D. Barnwell* and waited for a reply. Despite shuffling sounds emanating from behind the weather-beaten white wooden door, several seconds elapsed before a withered old man finally appeared.

"Yes?" he asked.

"Aloysius Vander Hopper." Creighton flashed his calling card case in hopes that it resembled a badge or whatever piece of identification private detectives carried. The elderly man squinted in bewilderment as the shiny object entered his range of vision and quickly disappeared. "I'm looking for a man by the name of Michael Barnwell. I believe he's staying here."

The man nodded and opened the door to allow Creighton admittance. The house was sealed up tightly—windows and doors shut and shades drawn—trapping the warm, humid summer air indoors. When his eyes had acclimated to the dim surroundings, Creighton noticed that the elderly man had been replaced by a younger, mustached version.

"Michael Barnwell?" Creighton presumed.

"Yeah. Who are you?"

Creighton tried the card case trick again, this time opening the case and closing it all with one deft motion. "Aloysius Vandufnuff-erhuf." Unable to recall the name he had previously provided, he slurred the last few syllables.

"No you're not," Barnwell stated bluntly. "Who are you, really?"

"A private detective. Your wife hired me."

"My wife doesn't have the money to hire—wait a minute—I know you. You're that guy I saw in the paper a few weeks back. You and some blonde solved those murder cases in Ridgebury. You're Craig Ashton."

"Close. It's Creighton Ashcroft… the third," he corrected, glad that someone had noticed his efforts in closing what had been described as Marjorie's cases. "And, yes, I did contribute to solving those crimes. Actually I—" Realizing that his boasts had put him in a dangerous situation, he stopped talking and tried on an ebullient smile.

"So why are you here? I haven't done anything."

"Like I said. Your wife hired me to find you." He rethought this approach since the newspaper made it clear that he and Marjorie worked pro bono. "Well, 'hire' isn't the correct word, since we don't charge for our services."

"We?" Barnwell quizzed.

"Marjorie McClelland and I. Marjorie's the blonde in the photo. She's my fiancée and my 'partner-in-crime.' Um, perhaps that wasn't the correct term to use… 'Partner-in-solving-crime'?"

Barnwell moved toward a window and peeked behind the shade. "Where is she right now?"

"I told her to take a walk. Told her that you and I had some business to discuss—man-to-man. I had a feeling you might think her presence here intrusive. After all, you know how women can be."

Barnwell relaxed a bit and moved back into the light of the foyer. "Yeah," he agreed. "Nagging and whining. Never happy with anything. When I met Elizabeth, she was great. Then we got married and I never did anything right. I never made enough money. I never did enough for her."

“Tell me about it,” Creighton commiserated. “My old lady’s always on my back. No matter what I do for her, it’s never enough.” He paused a moment, shocked, yet pleased, at how American his accent sounded. “Then, before you know it, there’s a kid on the way, and there’s two of them to please.”

“Yeah, Elizabeth had Michael Jr. and it was like I suddenly didn’t exist anymore. All she cared about was him.”

“Yeah, I couldn’t imagine if you added another kid into the mix.”

Barnwell took a step backward. “Another kid? I don’t … I don’t know what you mean.”

“Don’t you?” Creighton challenged.

“You know, don’t you? You know!” Barnwell shrieked.

Enough picking at it, Creighton thought. *It’s time to rip the bandage off.* “Know about what? The affair with Veronica Carter? The baby? The body in the cellar?”

The color ebbed from Barnwell’s face. “I didn’t do it! I swear!”

“Didn’t do what?” Creighton continued, feeling rather like Pat O’Brien in his latest film role. “Didn’t cheat on your wife with Veronica Carter, didn’t father her child, or didn’t kill her?”

“All of them … none of them …” Barnwell sounded as though he might burst into tears. “I didn’t kill her. I loved her.”

“Then you admit you had an affair with her.”

“Yes, but it started out innocent. I swear. I went to the Five O’Clock for lunch, where she waited tables. She was pretty, sure, but it was more than that. She listened. Really listened. Eventually I went there for coffee. For lunch. Every chance I got.”

“And the discussions became something more,” Creighton surmised.

"It wasn't my intent. It just 'happened.' I rented the bungalow as a place for Ronnie to stay and a place for us to meet. It was run-down, cheap, but we didn't care. Those were the happiest times of my life. Then ..."

"Then she told you she was having a baby," Creighton inserted.

Barnwell nodded somberly. "I was shocked and angry and scared. I already had a kid," his face hardened, "and there I was faced with another mouth to feed. I went nuts. Completely off my head. I stormed out and went to a local bar."

"Which one?"

Barnwell shook his head. "I don't remember. I was pretty well fractured by the time I left. The next thing I remember was waking up in my bed in Ridgebury with a splitting headache. I went to work that day, but I couldn't stop thinking about what had happened. I decided to see Ronnie. I knew she wasn't scheduled to work that day, so I checked at the bungalow. When I got there, the place was empty. Ronnie had cleared out her stuff, and I figured she had left for good. I was about to leave when I heard the faucet drip. I don't know why I thought of it, or why I even cared, except that my name was on the lease and I didn't want to be held accountable for damages, but I tried to turn off the tap. The shutoff valve in the bathroom was rusted solid, so I went into the cellar." His bottom lip trembled. "I swear to you she was dead when I got there! I swear!"

"I believe you," Creighton stated quietly. Inwardly, however, he was still uncertain. "I just have a few questions."

"Go ahead."

"When your wife came to us, she gave us the address of the bungalow written on a scrap of paper. She said she found it in your pocket. Now, I'm not a master of intrigue, but it seems that if you were trying to keep the bungalow a secret, that's not the sort of thing you'd carry around with you."

"I had written it down to give to a friend of mine—Gordon Merchant. We went to school together and now he works at Allied. He kept an eye on Elizabeth and the baby when I was with Ronnie. I planned on giving him the address so that he could reach me, in case of an emergency at home, but then everything happened." He chuckled. "Ironic isn't it? The emergency wasn't at home at all."

"And the key?" Creighton quizzed. "When Miss McClelland and I went to the bungalow, the cellar doors were locked. Are you trying to say that you stumbled upon your girlfriend's mutilated body and still had the presence of mind to lock the doors behind you and then slip the key back into your pocket?"

"I don't remember. I honestly don't remember, but I must have," Barnwell gushed. "I'm a tidy fellow, so it would make sense in a way if I had. But I really can't say for certain."

Creighton folded his arms across his chest. "There's also the matter of the suitcase."

"Suitcase?" Michael repeated.

"One of Veronica's suitcases was found under your desk at New England Allied Insurance. The interior of the suitcase was stained with blood. Veronica Carter's blood."

Michael Barnwell swayed to and fro as if he might collapse.

"Easy now," Creighton lent a steadying arm.

Barnwell rallied. "A bloodstained suitcase, you said? I have no idea where it came from. I know it sounds like I'm lying, but I'm not. I don't know anything about it."

"I don't think the police will buy that story. It has, if you'll pardon the expression, the crackle of confederate money about it."

"That's why I left and came here. When I found Ronnie's body, I knew the police would think I did it. I knew that Elizabeth would find out about the affair. I drove home and went to bed. That night, while Elizabeth was sleeping, I packed a small bag and made plans to leave town. I didn't know where else to go, except here. I know leaving makes me look guilty, but I didn't do it. I swear. Please, don't turn me in," Michael begged. "Please. You said yourself, the cops won't buy my story."

"No," Creighton agreed. "They probably won't. But running away only makes you look guiltier than if you were to step forward and tell the police everything you told me."

"They'll put me under arrest."

"Probably," Creighton conceded, "but, in the meantime, they'll check your story and eventually discover that it's true."

Barnwell was silent.

"Let's put it this way," Creighton approached the issue from a different tack, "at least you'll be able to see your wife and son. I know things would be a lot better for them if they could see you."

Barnwell rubbed his face exhaustedly. "All right, I'll go—if only to see my family. But if the cops don't check my story and find that I'm telling the truth, I don't know what I'll do."

"Don't worry," Creighton reassured as he took Barnwell by the arm. "If they don't look into your story, Marjorie and I will."

THIRTEEN

MARJORIE AND CREIGHTON WERE seated on Mrs. Patterson's front porch swing, sipping tea from delicate white china cups.

"You should have seen him, Mrs. Patterson," Marjorie boasted. "Creighton marched up to the front door, rang the buzzer, and emerged a few minutes later with Michael Barnwell in his custody. And now Barnwell's being held for obstruction of justice and suspicion of . . ." She suddenly recalled that she hadn't told Mrs. Patterson about the murder. ". . . kidnapping until we can investigate further. And it's all because of Creighton's efforts."

"How brave," Mrs. Patterson exclaimed as she tilted her rocking chair forward and selected a golden sugar cookie from a large jadeite platter.

Creighton examined the fingernails on his left hand and buffed them on the lapel of his summer-weight suit jacket. "Oh, it was nothing. I just appealed to his sense of reason."

"Really?" Marjorie challenged. "I heard you used a different approach."

"Oh?" Creighton asked innocently.

"Yes. I overheard Barnwell telling the story to Robert. Barnwell claims you tricked him into surrendering."

"Tricked him, did I? Well, I suppose I did outwit him in a way. It's difficult not to when you have a superior intellect like mine."

"Mmm," Marjorie grunted in agreement. "You did an excellent job. Especially when you complained about your nagging 'old lady.'" She arched a finely trimmed eyebrow. "I can only assume you were referring to me."

Creighton reared back in surprise. "Nooooooo," he nearly sang. "I mentioned an old lady, yes. But I wasn't referring to you."

Mrs. Patterson stopped rocking and chewing and leveled an "I dare you" glare at her male guest.

Creighton waved his arms frantically. "No no no no no! I would never say anything like that about you, Mrs. Patterson."

The elderly woman smiled complacently and went back to consuming her cookie, while rocking back and forth in her wicker chair.

"Then whom did you mean?"

"No one. I was merely trying to commiserate with Barnwell. Find common ground so he'd trust me and I could convince him to turn himself in peacefully. If I went in there boasting that I was going to marry the smartest, most beautiful girl in the world, he'd have punched me in the nose."

"That's quite the yarn you've spun there," Marjorie commented. "What do you think, Mrs. Patterson?"

"Yep. He's a smooth one all right." The older woman narrowed her eyes appraisingly. "But he's good looking and he seems to mean well. We'll let him off the hook … this time."

“That’s a nice ‘how do you do’ for apprehending a suspected mu-ehem, kidnapper,” he replied. “I hate to imagine what you would have done to me had I failed to bring him in.”

Mrs. Patterson drew a finger across her throat.

“Thanks, Mrs. P. I knew I could rely upon you.”

Mrs. Patterson smiled sweetly and sipped her tea.

“So,” Marjorie posed, “do you think Michael Barnwell’s guilty?”

“I don’t know. For Elizabeth’s sake, I’d like to think he isn’t,” Creighton replied. “But his story has more holes in it than—”

“—St. Andrew’s Golf Course,” Marjorie completed. “Yes I know.”

“I was going to say the woodwind section of the London Philharmonic,” he stated drily. “And what about you? Do you think he’s guilty?”

Marjorie poured herself a second cup of tea before responding. “Of … um, kidnapping … Veronica Carter? No, I don’t think he is.”

“But, darling,” Creighton argued, “what about the suitcase? It had Veronica Carter’s … fingerprints in it. I mean *on* it. And the key? You don’t honestly believe that story of his do you?”

“People do some very strange things when they’re panic-stricken. If Michael thought he might be considered a suspect, he’d certainly try to cover any signs that he had been in that cellar. As for the suitcase,” she sighed noisily. “It is pretty damning, isn’t it? And the one piece of evidence I can’t explain.”

Creighton nodded smugly. “Because there is no other explanation. Michael Barnwell mu-kidnapped Veronica Carter.”

“But when? Does he have an alibi for the time of the … kidnapping? He may not remember where he went after seeing Veronica, but someone might remember seeing him. And how did he ... manage to steal away with her? Did he beat her with his fists? Because if he did, he has no bruises or cuts on his hands. And what did he do with ... the rest of ... you know? These are things we need to find out before we can even discuss Michael Barnwell's innocence or guilt."

"I agree," Creighton concurred. "But don't be surprised if our findings don't point to Barnwell's innocence."

"I know I may be wrong, just as I know that what I'm about to say doesn't make much sense," Marjorie acknowledged. "However, my intuition tells me that there's more going on here than meets the eye."

"Far be it for me to second-guess your intuition, darling. I learned that lesson months ago. With that said, where should we start our investigation?"

"Veronica's friend, I think. If Mrs. Sullivan is right, Michael Barnwell might not have been the only man, um," she slid a self-conscious glance in Mrs. Patterson's direction, "um, taking Veronica to the movies."

"Yes, I seem to think Veronica's had her popcorn buttered before," Creighton cracked.

Marjorie piped in, "And perhaps at a few different theaters."

"If so, someone other than Michael Barnwell could have had a motive for the crime."

"And who more likely to know than Veronica's best friend? Close female friends tell each other everything," Marjorie asserted.

"Speaking of female friends, Marjorie," Mrs. Patterson seized the opportunity to change topic. "You don't have any close female friends to speak of. Who were you thinking of naming as your maid of honor?"

"I hadn't really thought of that," Marjorie confessed. "Do I need one? Can't Creighton and I be the only ones at the altar?"

"That's a good idea," Creighton agreed. "Truth be told, I can't think of anyone to ask as my best man either."

"But it looks so nice to have another couple at your side," Mrs. Patterson insisted. "A girl in a pretty summer dress and a handsome man in a suit would round things out nicely, especially in pictures."

"Why do I have a feeling that you've something, or more precisely, someone in mind?" Marjorie asked, suspicious of where this conversation was about to lead.

"Actually I do. Sharon and Robert are your age and they're friends … of sorts."

"A little too friendly, Mrs. P.," Creighton quipped. "Marjorie was engaged to Jameson just a few short months ago and the Schutts were trying to coax me into taking Sharon off their hands. Don't you think it's rather in bad form to ask a former … what's the term?"

"Sweetheart?" Marjorie offered.

"In the case of Jameson, yes. As far as Sharon goes, I was thinking more along the lines of 'captor,'" Creighton explained. "But, whatever you want to call it, I'm not sure it's in the best of taste to ask them to witness our nuptials."

"I agree," Marjorie chimed in. "Even if we were to ask them, I highly doubt they'd accept."

"I don't know about that," Mrs. Patterson opined. "And it may go far in mending fences."

"Oh no," Creighton uttered in dismay. "Mrs. P., what did you do? You already asked Sharon and Jameson, didn't you?"

"No," the elderly woman answered artlessly. "I did, however, mention it to Louise Schutt."

"Mrs. Schutt!" Marjorie nearly screamed. "She hates me! Sharon hates me too, for that matter. Always did, but even more so now that I'm marrying Creighton."

"Trust me, darling. I'm not exactly on their hit parade either," Creighton interjected.

"Actually, Marjorie, Louise seemed rather sympathetic toward you," Mrs. Patterson shrugged as if the concept was foreign to her as well. "I didn't get all the details, but apparently she's under the impression that Detective Jameson broke up with you in order to be with Sharon."

"Broke up with me?" Marjorie repeated incredulously. "To be with Sharon? Wherever did she get that idea?"

"Oh, these Schutts are so full of themselves." Creighton tried to sound casual. "Their heads are so big that Mr. Schutt should consider having the door on the bookshop widened." He gave a loud guffaw.

Marjorie, meanwhile, was lost in thought. "I broke off the engagement to be with you, Creighton. Unless, of course ..." her voice trailed off but then returned, louder than ever. "Unless of course Robert had been seeing Sharon all along and was waiting for me to break things off. He did seem to bounce back rather quickly."

"Bah," Creighton exclaimed. "You know Jameson. Slow reaction time."

"I suppose," Marjorie admitted. "Although I'm really not sure I want them to be our maid of honor and best man."

"Marjorie, dear," Mrs. Patterson reasoned. "That's all in the past. You have Creighton now and a full life ahead of you."

Marjorie beamed. "You're right. I'm being childish. All that matters is that I'm going to be Mrs. Creighton Ashcroft. What's past is past. Besides, Reverend Price said the wedding ceremony is only thirty minutes long. After that, we'll be at the reception and then our honeymoon."

"Umm, actually," Mrs. Patterson said timidly, "I spoke with Reverend Price today and there's a small problem. You see, he was under the impression that Creighton is a Presbyterian."

"No," Creighton corrected. "I'm Anglican."

"I thought so. And Marjorie's Catholic," the elderly woman added. "The church rules state that only members of the Presbyterian faith can be married in the church. Likewise, he feels strange about performing the ceremony when Father Callahan was the priest who baptized Marjorie and gave her first communion. So, he suggested you have the ceremony at St. Agnes."

Marjorie nodded. "All right. I suppose we'll see Father Callahan tomorrow."

"I already did."

"Oh? Was he fine with the idea?"

"Well, he was fine with marrying you, but he wasn't very keen about marrying you to Creighton. When I mentioned the fact that Creighton was Anglican, and more importantly, English, he broke into a chorus of 'A Nation Once Again.'"

"Oh dear," Marjorie exclaimed. "Poor Father Callahan. How old is he now? Seventy-five?"

"Eighty," Mrs. Patterson answered. "He truly is a sweet man, but I think it's time he retired. Perhaps considered going back to the old country."

Marjorie sighed. "So where does that leave us?"

"I don't know about you," Creighton remarked as he adjusted his tie nervously, "but it leaves me highly skeptical of any package with a return address of St. Agnes's Parish or Father Callahan."

"Don't be silly," Marjorie chided. "Father Callahan's harmless ... unless of course he's been drinking too much whiskey. Even then, however, the most he ever does is run along the village green in his nightshirt, fire his father's pistol in the air, and shout *'Erin go Bragh!'*"

Mrs. Patterson continued her account of the day's events. "After my visit with Father Callahan, I went back to see Reverend Price and explained what had happened. He said he'll perform the ceremony, but it can't be at the church. However, he was kind enough to offer the tent they use for the church fair."

"The red and white striped one?" Creighton asked.

"Yes, that's it."

"With the hole in it, from when Freddie accidently set off a roman candle last Fourth of July?" Marjorie inserted.

"The very same," Mrs. Patterson nodded. "My thought was that we could set it up on the fair grounds."

The Ridgebury fairgrounds lay between the First Presbyterian Church and the Ridgebury Cemetery. Green and verdant in spring, the grounds were reduced to a dirty, dusty wasteland by the end of the Annual Church Fair every June. Marjorie tried hard not to frown. As much as she had wished her father could be present at her wedding, she wasn't certain she wanted to hold the ceremony a stone's throw from his grave.

"Or, if you'd rather, we could put it on the village green. It might be nice, having the home you grew up in, right there, within view. The only problem with the village green is that the main road isn't paved, so if it rains any time near the wedding, it's muddy and filled with puddles. However, if it's dry, dust flies up whenever a car drives past. In either case, you'd have to be careful of your wedding gown. But at least, with the tent, if it rains, we're covered … so long as no one stands under the hole, of course."

Creighton imagined a circus tent set up on Ridgebury village green in the middle of a torrential rain storm, mud splashing up from passing vehicles and trucks. Then, alternatively, he imagined the whole of Ridgebury transformed into an Oklahoma Dust Bowl town; sand, dirt, and sagebrush blowing through the tent and coating the wedding party and guests with dust.

"You do realize we could have the wedding at Kensington House," he ventured.

"Oh no," Mrs. Patterson argued. "The point is for the whole community to come together and make a wedding, so that the bride and groom have not a care in the world."

Marjorie and Creighton nodded and replied in unison, "Ah."

"Before I forget," Mrs. Patterson said breathlessly, "you two need to meet with Reverend Price to discuss the ceremony. I think he has something special planned!"

Again, Marjorie and Creighton nodded and replied in unison, "Ah."

"I'm sure we can work something in either tomorrow or the day after." Creighton placed his cup and saucer on the table and stretched broadly. "In the meantime, it sounds like we have a long day ahead of us. What time is it, Marjorie?"

She glanced at her watch. "Five minutes to nine."

"Hey, maybe I can take you to the movies. There's a James Cagney/Pat O'Brien film playing. For some reason, I have the urge to go see it. And, perhaps we could get some buttered popcorn?" He winked at Marjorie, rose to his feet, and bestowed upon their hostess a small kiss on the cheek. "Wonderful dinner as usual, Mrs. P. Thank you, and don't forget, tomorrow you're my guest."

Marjorie followed Creighton's lead. "That's right. Tomorrow you get to sit back and get treated like a queen."

"Oh, that's not necessary," she blushed. "I like cooking for you kids, besides it's nice not having to eat alone. Although someone else doing the cooking and cleaning up will give Marjorie and me a chance to look over those dress patterns. Oh, you'll be such a beautiful bride, Marjorie!"

"Thank you," Marjorie said with tears welling up in her eyes. "For everything."

"Never you mind," Mrs. Patterson dismissed. "You two run along and rest up for your big day of detective work."

The couple hurried down the porch steps and toward the slate walkway under Mrs. Patterson's motherly gaze. When they were out of earshot, she said to herself quietly, "'Taking her to the movies.' How old do they think I am?"

FOURTEEN

Creighton and Marjorie lay on lounge chairs by the pool outside Kensington House, gazing at the stars.

"A tent with red and white stripes," Creighton remarked. "What's next? Circus music playing as you walk down the aisle?"

Marjorie convulsed in laughter. "Creighton, darling, Mrs. Patterson's doing her best," she excused upon catching her breath.

"I know she is," he acknowledged, "but that doesn't mean we should agree to having Jameson and Sharon as the best man and maid of honor. Nor does it mean we should agree to Chinese water torture being performed upon our guests."

Marjorie shook her head and chuckled. "It's too ridiculous for words, isn't it? My former fiancé as best man. Your pursuer—and my biggest detractor—as maid of honor. A cast of one hundred extras and, in a cameo appearance, a leaky tent."

"It's like a Cecil B. DeMille film set in New England and without the usual Cecil B. DeMille budget." Creighton rose from his chair and poured himself and Marjorie each a glass of brandy.

Marjorie sighed. "I wish we could convince them to hold the wedding here. It's so beautiful and peaceful."

"Not to mention private," Creighton added. He handed Marjorie her glass of brandy and settled in beside her. "Cold, darling?"

"A little," she confessed.

He removed his jacket and draped it over her shoulders. "I can think of a few ways to warm you up."

"I'm sure you can," Marjorie purred.

"Why, Miss McClelland, you naughty thing. I was talking about going indoors."

"Of course you were. Especially after your movie and popcorn comments."

Creighton raised his eyebrows and pulled his fiancée closer. "We could snuggle by the fire."

"It's cool outside," she conceded, "but I'm not sure we need a fire. That might be a little too warm."

"Well then, we'll just have to remove some of these clothes ..."

She laughed and kissed him. "It is a little cold, but that doesn't mean—"

"Of course not, darling." He smirked. "Let's go inside." He rose from the chaise lounge and lent Marjorie a hand. "You know, I'm very glad you want to have the wedding here. It means that you feel like this is home. Your home. After what happened months ago, I doubted you'd ever feel comfortable here."

"It was a bit difficult at first," she admitted, "but then I realized that the house wasn't what shot me. It may sound silly, but if anything, the house gave me the strength to protect Mary Stafford. And it gave her the courage to escape. It's a happy house, Creighton. There've been too many beginnings here for it to be otherwise."

Creighton's eyes misted over. "I never thanked God for anything as much as when you survived that ordeal. I don't know where I'd be right now if you hadn't."

"You have nothing to worry about, Creighton. We'll be living here for a long time. Barbecues in the summer. Christmases with lots of snow for sledding. Easter egg hunts in the backyard. Big, old-fashioned bon fires in the autumn ..."

"And, years from now, a little boy like Michael Jr., with green eyes, blonde hair, and my sweet disposition—"

"Don't you mean my sweet disposition?"

"Your sweet disposition? No wonder you write fiction."

Marjorie slugged him in the arm.

"I rest my case." Then the smile on his face changed into something softer—an expression less like a smirk and more like one of pride. "I can see him now. He'll be learning to swim in the pool, opening Christmas presents, eating the chocolate eggs in his Easter basket, leaping into giant piles of leaves." He gave Marjorie a kiss on the forehead as they walked into the study. "Loving his mum as much as I do."

"Oh please. We both know you'd be the fun parent—chasing him around the house on roller skates, teaching him to play practical jokes on me. He'd love you just as much as he loves me—possibly more since you'd be a pal as well as a parent. Just look at Michael Jr.: he's been simply inconsolable without his father." She paused. "Reminds me of myself. I adored my father. Of course, my mother wasn't around when I was young, but even if she had been around, I think I still would have adored him. I may have gone through a 'mama' phase like most toddlers, but my father was such a kind, loving person, I don't think anything could have altered my feelings. Does that sound silly?"

"Not at all. I know I was closer to my mother when I was a young lad," Creighton added. "My mother only lived until I was about nine, but she was always there for me during those years. Even when she was ill and confined to bed, I'd come home from school and go straight to her bedroom to tell her about my lessons and the latest schoolyard gossip. But then again, I, like you, didn't have another option. My father wasn't what you'd call the typical parent. He was self-centered. God knows he never granted me a word of praise. Never bothered to ask how my day was. It was only natural that I should gravitate to a compassionate soul like my mother, just as you gravitated to your father. I like to think they're watching over us now, Marjorie, and that they're happy we've found each other. That's the strength you felt that evening. That's the strength that kept you and Mary alive… that's the strength that brought you back to me. And I'll never let you go again," he promised.

Creighton sat down upon the sofa and guided Marjorie onto the cushion beside him. There was no need to light a fire.

FIFTEEN

CREIGHTON AND MARJORIE TOOK advantage of the beautiful August morning to make the jaunt through the Connecticut countryside to downtown Hartford. After securing a spot in which to park the Phantom, they approached the dilapidated tenement building and climbed the rickety stairs to the third floor.

Inside the run-down apartment, Diana Hoffman lit a cigarette and draped her willowy frame artistically across the only piece of furniture in the room: a threadbare apricot-colored chaise lounge. "I don't know what I could possibly tell you about Ronnie Carter."

"I'm surprised," Marjorie reasoned. "After all, you two are friends, aren't you?"

"Best friends. But I still don't know what you expect me to tell you." She tilted her head back and exhaled a puff of white smoke.

"For starters, you might mention that she's been missing for the past three days," Creighton suggested.

Diana shrugged, causing her red satin kimono to slide off one shoulder. "Ronnie's always taking off in search of greener pastures.

She always comes back though—after finding that the green she saw in the distance was spinach." She took another drag on the cigarette and then exhaled. "Is that why you're here? Her boss reported her missing?"

"No, nothing like that. You see, Veronica Carter is dead."

Diana Hoffman's face showed no emotion as she sat up and snuffed her cigarette into a glass ashtray that sat on the floor. "Dead? How?"

"She was beaten to death," Marjorie replied.

Diana lit another cigarette and leaned back. "That's too bad. Mind you, I'm not surprised it happened. She never did know how to pick the good ones."

"And you do?" Creighton spoke up.

"Of course," she answered with more than a hint of sarcasm in her voice. "Why, just look at what my man's done for me." She gestured broadly at the shabby cold-water flat in which Marjorie and Creighton now stood. "I only waitress down at the bar every night because I'm bored."

"I'm sorry," Creighton apologized. "I didn't mean to offend you, Mrs.—"

"Save the 'Mrs.' It's *Miss* Hoffman. I'm not married." Her heavily madeup blue eyes narrowed. "Unless you'd like to change that, dreamboat."

Creighton cleared his throat and struggled to remain professional. "Um, thanks, but Marjorie and I ..."

She gave the writer a brief assessment. "Too bad. If it doesn't work out, give me a call."

"Sure, I'll keep you—" He caught a glimpse of Marjorie's frosty stare. "I don't think that will be necessary."

Marjorie nodded in silent approval. "When was the last time you saw Veronica—er—Ronnie Carter?"

"A week ago. My old man was working the graveyard shift. Ronnie and me decided to go down to Bruno's to have some fun."

"Bruno's?" Creighton repeated.

"It's a nightclub a few blocks from here," Diana explained.

"And that was the last time you saw her?"

"Yep."

"You didn't speak to her after that?" Marjorie asked.

"No. She was scheduled to work the day shift, and I always work nights. We said we'd call each other this Sunday. It's our day off."

"Miss Hoffman, what do you know about Michael Barnwell?"

"Barnwell? Never heard of the—oh wait. Is that the last name of the guy Ronnie was seeing?"

"Yes, it is," Marjorie confirmed.

"Tall guy? Mustache? Works in insurance?"

"That's the one," Creighton attested.

"Yeah, Ronnie never told me his last name. Only went on and on about her 'Mikey' and how the two of them were going to run off together and get married and live happily ever after." She extinguished her cigarette and shook her platinum-blonde head. "When the waitress from the Five O'Clock called looking for her, I thought maybe they did elope after all. I should have known better. Stuff like that never happens to girls like me and Ronnie."

"Ronnie should have known better too," Creighton opined. "Barnwell has a wife and young son."

"He's married?" Diana sighed, "It figures. Last guy she got mixed up with was married too."

"Do you think Veronica knew Barnwell was married?" Marjorie posed.

Diana fished another cigarette from the box on her lap. "Hard to say. But if she did know, it wouldn't have put her off any. In fact, I'd say she enjoyed the challenge."

"Ronnie's neighbor reported hearing Ronnie and a man arguing the night the murder took place," Marjorie prefaced. "Can you think of any reason the two of them might have argued? Anything that might have caused Michael to become violent?"

"Nope. From what I could tell, Ronnie was happy. Very happy." She placed the cigarette between her lips and retrieved a lighter from the pocket of her kimono.

"Did you know that Ronnie was pregnant?"

Diana had been in the process of lighting her cigarette. When Marjorie delivered this bit of news, Diana's jaw dropped open, allowing the unlit cigarette to fall from her lips and onto the floor. "Pregnant?"

"The doctor discovered it while performing the autopsy," Creighton explained.

"Pregnant. But she—I'm her best friend. She didn't say anything when I saw her."

"She might not have had the chance," Creighton theorized. "She may have been waiting to tell Michael first and when she did ..." his voice trailed off.

"You think Michael killed her because she was pregnant?"

"We believe he might have," Marjorie affirmed. "Unless you can convince us otherwise."

She selected another cigarette from the box, placed it between her lips and, this time, made certain to light it quickly. "Nope. I told you already, I never met Michael Barnwell. It's just… it's just when you told me that Ronnie was dead, I immediately assumed that Trent Taylor was responsible somehow."

"Trent Taylor?"

"The last guy Ronnie was mixed up with. The married guy I told you about. He and Ronnie were seeing each other for the better part of the year. He strung her along, saying that if it weren't for his wife, he'd marry her. Well, the man upstairs must have heard him and decided to call his bluff, 'cause what do you know? She dropped dead from some stomach thing. Begins with a *g*."

"Gastritis?" Marjorie guessed.

"That's it." Miss Hoffman sat up and swung her legs over the side of the chaise lounge. "So the old lady dies of this gas-gas—"

"Gastritis," Marjorie inserted.

"Right. And what does he tell Ronnie? He says he wants things to stay the way they've always been because it's too soon after his wife's death to remarry. Can you believe the heel?"

"That's a heel all right," Marjorie agreed. "But I fail to see how he had a motive for murdering Ronnie."

"I'm getting there." She drew a puff off her cigarette and quickly exhaled. "Ronnie was devastated. Though I can't say she didn't have it coming to her—stealing another woman's man like she did." Diana stared off into the distance.

"You were saying," Creighton prompted, "you think Trent had something to do with Ronnie's death."

"I don't think he had something to do with it. I know he did, and I'll tell you how I know," Diana averred. "Ronnie was brokenhearted when Trent told her he wouldn't marry her. Came crying on my doorstep one night. I told her to dump the guy. She didn't want to at first. Like I said, once Ronnie fell for a guy, she had a tough time cutting 'im loose—but she finally agreed. She went to see Trent the next morning and do you know what happened? He smacked her one, right in the jaw, and accused her of throwing him over for another man! Can you believe it?"

"Was she seeing someone else?" Marjorie inquired.

Diana shook her head. "No, Ronnie didn't even look at another guy the time she was with Trent. But that didn't matter to him. Do you know the last thing he said to her that day? He said, 'If I catch you with another guy, I'll kill you.'"

Creighton spoke up. "Men have been known to hurl all sorts of threats and accusations when women leave them, but most of them don't make good on their words."

"That's what I thought too—at first. But then Ronnie told me something that made me take his threats seriously."

"What's that?"

"She told me that Trent Taylor murdered his wife."

"I thought she died of gastritis," Marjorie pointed out.

"That's what everyone was supposed to think," Diana said. "The truth is, it was poison."

"And the coroner didn't find this poison?" Creighton asked skeptically.

"He didn't look. Mrs. Taylor had never been a well woman. Bleeding ulcers, liver problems, you name it, she had it. If she was to die of ga ... ga ... ga ..."

"Gastritis," Marjorie offered yet again.

"... No one would have thought otherwise."

"I'm confused," Creighton announced. "If Trent had no intention of marrying Ronnie, why would he murder his wife?"

Diana had been so wrapped up in the story she was telling, nearly two minutes had elapsed since her last cigarette. She quickly rectified the situation. "A few reasons," she stated as smoke exited her nostrils in long, sinuous tendrils. "First, Mrs. Taylor was a cow. She was a sick woman who didn't suffer her illnesses silently. She ran her husband ragged. It was always 'Trent, get me this' and 'Trent, get me that.' Who wouldn't want to bump off someone like that? Especially when there's a large life insurance policy to sweeten the pot." She propped her feet up on the chaise and leaned on one elbow.

"Did Ronnie discuss these allegations with anyone else?" Marjorie quizzed.

"No, not that I'm aware of."

"Did she produce any evidence to substantiate the story?"

"No."

"And yet you believed her. Why?"

Diana Hoffman ground her cigarette angrily into the ashtray. "Because, Miss McClelland," she shouted, "she was my friend. She was never one to scare easily, yet she was terrified of Trent Taylor. Now if you and Mr. Ashcroft are finished trying to tarnish my friend's memory, I have to get ready for work. You can let yourselves out." With that, she stomped off to the bedroom and slammed the door behind her.

SIXTEEN

TRENT TAYLOR'S AUTO REPAIR shop was located on Farmington Avenue in the area known as Nook Farm. Once a fashionable neighborhood that could boast authors Mark Twain and Harriet Beecher Stowe among its residents, the area, like the rest of America, now faced harder times. Many of the large Victorian homes lay dormant. Others were in a state of disrepair. And still others had been converted into apartment buildings and boarding houses, their metallic exoskeletons of fire escapes a far cry from the wisteria and ivy that once clung to their elegant façades.

Creighton pulled the Phantom into an unpaved lot and parked it beside a familiar police car.

"Funny running into you," Jameson taunted as Marjorie and Creighton emerged from the Phantom.

"Not too funny. You've been following us ever since we left Diana Hoffman's apartment," Creighton replied.

"Afraid you'd miss something?" Marjorie jeered.

"No, I'd be interviewing Trent Taylor whether you were here or not," Jameson stated.

"But you'd be interviewing him just a little bit later, perhaps," Creighton asserted cheekily.

"I went to Diana Carter's apartment, and, as fate would have it, I saw you driving away, just as I was pulling up to the building. A stroke of good luck for me, unless you don't want me present during this interview."

"No," Marjorie answered honestly. "You're more than welcome to join us. After all, clues are clues and testimony is testimony. The real skill lies in fitting those pieces together to form a complete picture. But what matters most is that we catch the killer. Come on," she waved.

Jameson followed her and Creighton across the street and through one of the repair shop's open bay doors. A tall, well-built man with reddish-blonde hair greeted them.

Jameson flashed his badge. "Detective Robert Jameson, Hartford County Police. These are my associates, Miss McClelland and Mr. Ashcroft."

Creighton nodded once in acknowledgment. "We're looking for Mr. Taylor."

The man wiped the grease from one hand and extended it in greeting. "You've found him. What can I do for you?"

"We're looking for information regarding Veronica Carter. Her friend, Diana Hoffman referred us to you."

"Good old Diana." Trent smirked. "How is she?"

"Er, she's in ... high spirits," the Englishman said reluctantly.

"High spirits?" Taylor laughed. "Well, Diana always did have a bad temper. And Veronica? What's she been up to?"

Jameson glanced at the other two mechanics in the shop. "Mr. Taylor, is there somewhere more private where we can talk?"

Trent followed his gaze. "Sure, let's go into the office."

He led the trio to a small room furnished with a shabby desk and chair and decorated with magazine pinups. He gestured to Marjorie to take the seat while he plopped himself on the corner of the desk. "So, what's this all about?"

Jameson was the first to respond. "Veronica Carter is dead."

"Taking the gentle approach again, I see," Creighton murmured.

"Dead? You're kidding."

"I'm afraid not, Mr. Taylor."

Trent was visibly upset. "Ronnie? Poor kid." He shook his head slowly. "How did it happen?"

"She was murdered," Marjorie answered. "Beaten to death."

"Did you catch the guy?"

"That's why we're here," Jameson stated.

Taylor leapt to his feet. "Hey, you don't think I had anything to do with it, do you?"

The detective begged the question. "What do you know about Michael Barnwell?"

"Never heard of the guy. Why?"

"He was Ronnie's latest squeeze. That's why."

"Good for him. Hope she simmered down a bit since I knew her. She was a handful, boy." He slapped his knee and guffawed loudly. "A real handful, let me tell you!"

"That's an excellent idea," Creighton noted. "Why don't you tell us?"

Trent sat back on the desk. "Where do I start? Ronnie was a cute kid. Brunette, pretty face, great pins—"

"Pardon me, 'pins'?" Creighton interrupted.

"Sorry, legs. She had great legs. Say, where'd you find this guy?" he whispered to the other occupants in the room.

"I traded my Green Stamps for a Fair Isle 'knit,'" Marjorie shrugged. "Ended up being a typo."

"Knit?" Taylor repeated obtusely.

"It's a pun," Marjorie explained.

"Punt? That's a football term." He grinned. "You like football, doll face? Because I can—"

Creighton cleared his throat noisily. "Your wife, Mr. Taylor. What about your wife?"

"My wife?" Taylor asked.

"Yes. Your wife was a sick woman," Jameson started.

"Oh yeah! Yeah, my wife was a sick woman. She couldn't get around the way she used to, and Ronnie ... well, Ronnie was fun. Full of life. We started seeing each other, but I made it clear that I wasn't going to divorce Cynthia. I loved her and I promised I would never leave her. I knew Ronnie wanted me to marry her, but I made it clear from the start that was never gonna happen."

"Pardon my skepticism, but refusing to marry Ronnie Carter doesn't mitigate the fact that you had an affair with her. And, quite honestly, if you were so devoted to your wife, I'm not sure you would have been able to carry off an affair with Ronnie Carter," Jameson prodded. "Not without your conscience getting in the way."

"Hey, it's easy for you to say. You didn't live with Cynthia," Taylor challenged. "I took care of her every need. She needed a bath—I gave her a bath. She couldn't get into bed—I helped her into bed. Anything she asked for, I gave it to her. Anything she needed—I went out of my way to get it. She couldn't stand very long by the stove, so I cooked. Pushing a mop around was exhausting, so I cleaned. And aside from all of that, I ran this place to pay for her medicine."

"Sounds like that in itself is a motive for murder," Creighton opined.

"Murder? Where'd you get that from? I was devoted to her."

"Devoted, yes. However, your wife's death would set you free from the role of caretaker. And that life insurance policy of hers might not have been able to buy back the years you'd lost, but I'm sure it eased your pain," Creighton baited.

"What are you talking about?" Trent's voice rose several octaves. "I didn't get a dime from Cynthia's life insurance policy. When I broke up with Ronnie, she went to the insurance company and disputed my claim. She told them I poisoned my wife. The company won't pay out until they've investigated the case."

"Ronnie went to the insurance company," Creighton repeated.

"When *you* broke up with Ronnie?" Marjorie exclaimed at the same time as Creighton.

Detective Jameson and Trent Taylor stood with their mouths agape.

"Go ahead, darling," Creighton spurred his fiancée onward. "I'll pick up where you leave off."

Marjorie nodded. "Diana Hoffman had it the other way around. She said that Ronnie broke it off with you."

"Broke up with me? Are you kidding?"

Jameson cleared his throat. "Look, Mr. Taylor, I know it may be difficult to admit—"

"Admit that Ronnie left me? I would if it was true, but it's not. Believe me, by the end, I was happy to see her go, but the kid kept hanging on—calling here at the shop, showing up on my doorstep at all hours. I know she and me had been an item before and that she expected marriage once I was free, but my wife had just died. I wasn't ready to marry someone else."

"Did you tell that to Ronnie?"

"I tried to, but she went berserk. She started hitting and kicking me like I was a bum or even worse."

Marjorie spoke up. "Most women would be upset to find out you had strung them along."

"I didn't string her along. Maybe she got her hopes up, but I was honest from the get-go. It was fun and it was her idea in the first place—not mine. She knew I was married when we met, but she wouldn't take no for an answer. I gave in—I mean she wasn't a bad-looking girl. But marriage? Naw, she wasn't the kind of girl a guy marries, if you know what I mean."

"No," Marjorie stated naïvely. "I don't know what you mean."

The men looked at each other as if trying to decide who was going to draw the shortest straw.

Trent took a shot. "Well," he began, "for starters, she was fast. Second, she was mean. And last, she was a bigger nut bar than an Oh Henry!"

"O. Henry? He's a short story writer, isn't he?" Creighton ventured.

"Not this time, sweetness," Marjorie corrected. "An Oh Henry! is a candy bar. A candy bar filled with peanuts."

"Yeah," Trent nodded. "Yeah ... where was I?"

Jameson shook his head. "I have no idea anymore."

"I do," Creighton declared. "How can you be certain that Ronnie was the reason your claim was denied?"

"Because she threatened me," Trent pronounced. "She told me if I broke things off with her, she would go to the cops and the insurance company and tell them that I poisoned Cynthia." He paused and a wide grin spanned his boyish countenance. "I guess the cops saw she was crazy and sent her away. But the insurance company ... well, they believed her. Must have or my claim would have been good. Unless ..."

"Unless?"

"Diana Hoffman's had it out for me since I chose Ronnie over her."

"Beg pardon?" Marjorie couldn't believe her ears at first, but then she recalled Diana's comment about Veronica 'getting what she deserved' for stealing another woman's man. She had naturally assumed that Cynthia Taylor was the betrayed woman in question.

"I knew Diana before I even met Ronnie. Diana was the better-looking of the two, but she was hard. She was harder than a three penny nail, but I can't blame her. Every man she ever met did her wrong, including her own father. Who wouldn't turn hard after that? Who wouldn't turn mean?" His eyes grew dull, lifeless. "I didn't choose Ronnie to hurt Diana. Honest I didn't. Ronnie was just ... different. And Diana hated her for it. She hated me too, for choosing Ronnie. She would have done anything to spite us. Anything."

"Including murdering Ronnie?" Marjorie asked.

"I hate to say it, but yes. Yes, she might have if she was angry enough. She has a terrible temper."

"And disputing your insurance claim?"

"Absolutely. If Ronnie had gone to her and lied about me ... yeah, Diana would have disputed my claim."

"Well, if she did, there's one way to find out," Creighton stated. "Mr. Taylor, who's handling your wife's policy?"

Trent took a moment to reply, but Marjorie and Creighton already anticipated the answer. "New England Allied."

SEVENTEEN

MARJORIE MCCLELLAND LED HER male companions up the granite steps of the art deco building designed by Lockwood, Greene and Company. She entered the elevator and pressed number 12.

The doors opened on the New England Allied Insurance Company. This time, however, the secretary in the tweed suit was not there to greet them.

"Hmmm," Marjorie remarked. "Should we just go on in?"

A tanned man with light blonde hair and an athletic build appeared on the scene. "Excuse me, are you Miss McClelland?"

"Yes, I am."

"I'm Gordon Merchant, Michael's friend. He told me you might come by." He extended his hand to Creighton.

"Creighton Ashcroft," the Englishman shook hands and introduced himself. "And this is Detective Jameson with the Hartford County Police."

Jameson tipped his hat in greeting.

"Oh, I had no idea the police would be joining you." He smiled nervously.

"This is a murder investigation," Marjorie explained.

"True enough. I guess I just assumed since they had Michael, their part was all over. At least that's what Michael said. He told me about you, Mr. Ashcroft, and how you and Miss McClelland would come here, but he didn't think the cops would put enough stock in his story to follow up on it."

"When it comes to murder, the Hartford County Police Department is obliged to its citizens to follow every lead to the end," Jameson pontificated.

Marjorie licked an index finger and raised it as if to measure air velocity. "It's awfully windy all of a sudden."

Gordon's eyebrows furrowed in confusion. "Unless you'd like to see Michael's desk again, there's a meeting room we can use. It's a lot more private than talking here."

"It's pretty private right now," Marjorie noted. "Just the four of us."

"That's because Helen, our receptionist, is on break. Everyone here gets fifteen minutes for break and thirty minutes for lunch. Although, if you ask me, Helen seems to sneak a little extra time."

Merchant directed them to a room with a round table and four chairs. He shut the door quietly behind them and took the seat opposite Marjorie. "I want you to know that I'm here to help you any way I can."

"Good," Jameson proclaimed. "Then perhaps you can tell us what case Michael was working on before he went to Springfield."

The question gave Gordon Merchant pause. "I'm afraid I can't tell you that. It's confidential."

"Off the record," Jameson assured. "We'll find out anyway, once we get a warrant to search the company records."

Gordon remained silent.

"Listen," Jameson pressed, "I'm giving you a chance to help your friend get back home."

"Is he as close as that to getting out? Michael, I mean?"

"Close? No, I wouldn't say that. I wouldn't say that at all. In fact, at this moment he's looking very guilty."

"Then why should I do anything?" Gordon asked. "Why should I do or say anything if it won't help Elizabeth and the baby?"

Marjorie stepped in. "Michael told us that he asked you to keep an eye on his wife and child while he was with Veronica Carter. I can understand your sense of responsibility."

"He did and I'm sorry I agreed to it. Pretending he was at my place playing poker when all the while he was at that bungalow with Veronica. It makes me sick to think I lied for him. It makes me sick to think I lied to a woman like Elizabeth. It's wrong the way he treats her. Everything she does is for her family and he never appreciates it. She cooks his meals, keeps an immaculate house, darns his socks, and takes care of his son. And all he does is complain about how she keeps him from achieving his dreams. Dreams," he whispered. "For guys like me, having a wife and a son like Mike has is the dream. A house in a quiet neighborhood, a nice little wife, a healthy kid ... what more could a guy ask for? Michael Barnwell was living the dream, and yet it wasn't enough. He wanted more."

"More?" Creighton probed.

Gordon nodded. "Mike's a bright guy. Exceptionally bright. He's always felt he could do better than this place. We all do, I guess, but for Mike, it really stuck in his craw that he had to work for someone else. He's always felt that New England Allied was mismanaged—and maybe it is—but Mike believes he could do a better job running it."

"Lots of people feel that way," Creighton commented. "But if you offer them the opportunity to take control of the reins, they don't want the responsibility."

"That's where Mike's different," Merchant explained. "He does want the responsibility. He wants the power. He'd give his eyeteeth for it. If he could get a good price for it, he'd sell that house of his, move his family into an apartment, and invest the money in his own business."

"Is Elizabeth aware of his ambitions?

"Oh yeah. They argue about it all the time. Elizabeth doesn't think Michael should be gambling with their son's future. She says it's a father's responsibility to make sure his child has a roof over his head and food in his stomach. Everything else comes second. Michael views it as her trying to hold him back."

"And you?" Marjorie prompted. "What do you think?"

"I think she's being a good mother. She's doing her best to protect her family. Her top priority is her son—that's how it should be. A mother should watch over her child, and truth is, that's the way it really needs to be with a guy like Mike. Don't get me wrong, he's great and all, but once he gets it in his head to do something, he doesn't let anything get in his way. Elizabeth's strong—she knows she has to be or he'll walk all over her." He paused. "I don't know why I've been beating around the bush here. I mean I know Michael's my friend, but if he's done something that could get me in trouble, then I need to cut him loose."

"What do you mean, Mr. Merchant?" Marjorie inquired.

"I mean that, well... by now I'm sure you figured out that Mike was working on the Taylor case."

"We suspected it, yes," Creighton admitted.

"Well, that's how he and Veronica met."

"Michael told us they met at the Five O'Clock," Jameson stated.

"Nah. The first time they laid eyes on each other was in this office. After that, Mike would go down to the Five O'Clock and visit Veronica during her shift. But the initial meeting? Right here."

"What was Veronica doing here?"

Gordon chuckled. "She came in to rat out her former boyfriend. She had already been to the police, but they didn't want anything to do with it. Thought she was a crackpot. I mean, what kind of woman goes around town telling people that a guy murdered his wife? I thought she was a crackpot too when she first came in here. But for Mikey, it was love at first sight. Mike thought she was the bravest little thing on two legs. And Veronica? Well, she hung on Mike's every word. She listened to his plans and dreams and even his stupid ideas. Mike needs that. He needs someone to listen. Elizabeth used to listen, but now... now I think she's just tired. I think she thought he'd outgrow a lot of his foolishness once the baby came. I think she thought he'd settle down more, but that's just not Mikey."

"Did Elizabeth know about the affair?"

"No, I don't think she did. Well, not directly. I think she knew something was going on, although she wasn't sure exactly what."

Marjorie knew the question would upset Gordon, but she had to ask it. "If Elizabeth had found out about the affair, do you think she could have murdered Veronica Carter?"

"Never," he insisted. "Never! Elizabeth doesn't have an unkind bone in her body. She's an excellent mother, a wonderful wife, and an all-around great girl."

"What about Michael? Do you believe he could have murdered Veronica Carter?"

Gordon hesitated. "If you mean *do I think he's capable*—yes. If you mean *do I think he actually did it*—no. He had no reason to. He was crazy about Veronica."

"What if Veronica were pregnant?" Creighton posed.

"Preg—was she? Was Veronica going to have a baby?"

Creighton nodded.

"Then yeah. Yeah, that definitely would have knocked him for a loop. It would have been Elizabeth all over again. See, Elizabeth and Michael got married 'under the gun' so to speak. And he resented her. No matter what Elizabeth did, she could never live that down. Mike was always saying how she trapped him, how she ruined his life." Gordon shook his head. "Poor Elizabeth. It killed her when he talked like that."

Marjorie looked Gordon Merchant straight in the eye. "You might think me too bold to ask this, but I have to check."

"Go ahead."

"You're in love with Elizabeth Barnwell, aren't you?"

Gordon bit his bottom lip and nodded slowly. "I would give anything if she were my wife instead of Michael Barnwell's. Anything."

EIGHTEEN

AFTER THEIR INTERROGATION OF Gordon Merchant, Creighton and Marjorie said goodbye to Detective Jameson and traveled back to Ridgebury to pay a visit to Reverend Price. They arrived to find the white-haired cleric seated at his desk, perusing a copy of Marjorie McClelland's *Homicide in Hungary*.

When he saw the young couple, he shut the book and rose to his feet to greet them. "Marjorie. Creighton."

Marjorie gave the minister a hug and then stepped aside so that the two men could shake hands. "How are you?" she inquired.

"Excited," he answered. "And very happy to see you. How are you children doing?"

"Oh, we're fine," Creighton replied. "Engaging in some reading there, Vicar?"

Price laughed. "I read it when it was first released, but it's my favorite. I find it ... *inspiring*."

"Inspiring? You're not planning on pushing someone onto the tracks at the Ridgebury Railroad Station are you?" Marjorie asked.

The Reverend's mouth formed the shape of a tiny *o*. "Oh no," he chuckled. "Nothing like that. It was going to be a surprise, in fact, but now that you're here, I may as well tell you." He gestured them to be seated.

"Mrs. Patterson did say you were cooking up something special for our wedding," Marjorie acknowledged as she sat in one of the two carved wooden chairs that faced the minister's desk. "She didn't say what it was, mind you. But she did tell us you were up to something."

"Oh that Emily," he waved a scolding finger. "I knew she couldn't keep a secret if her life depended on it, that's why I didn't give her any of the details. I figured if anyone was going to spill the beans, it was going to be me."

"We're all ears," Creighton urged.

"Yes, go on and tell us," Marjorie egged him on.

Reverend Price lifted the cover of *Homicide in Hungary* and extracted the sheet of scrap paper he had placed there for safekeeping. "Marjorie, you and I have known each other for quite a while now. By virtue of being a member of the community, I've had the opportunity to watch you grow from a little girl into a beautiful young woman. However, it wasn't until you became an author that you and I found we had quite a bit in common: namely, murder. I had always been a fan of mystery novels, but your books have truly been an eye-opening experience. Because of my admiration for your work, I want your ceremony to be as unique and memorable as you are."

Marjorie smiled, "Why, thank you, Reverend. That's very kind of you to say."

"It's not kindness. It's the truth. However, as I am a minister, the heart of the ceremony will be spiritual, dignified, with a little twist at the end—just like Marjorie's books."

"Well, you've piqued my interest," Creighton confessed.

"Good. I'll give you a brief overview of the ceremony I envisioned." Price referred to his notes. "Creighton, you will be at the altar—"

"We're getting married beneath the tent you're loaning us," Creighton pointed out. "There is no altar."

"Yes, that's a very good point." Price scratched out an item on his list. "So, you will be standing at the front of the tent with your best man. Emily mentioned that you had asked Detective Jameson to stand up for you."

Creighton winced. "Not exactly. I'm still undecided."

Reverend Price jotted this information onto the scrap paper. "While you and your best man—whomever he may be—are at the front of the tent, the music will start." He looked up from his notes. "Since you're not getting married in the church, we don't have the luxury of using the organ. But my secretary, Mrs. Reynolds, has kindly volunteered the use of her wind-up phonograph."

"How nice of her. Does she have Mendelssohn's 'Wedding March'?" Marjorie inquired.

"Unfortunately no, but we have been able to locate a very good, scratch-free copy of 'Alice Blue Gown.'"

Marjorie's jaw dropped.

"That's a lovely song," Creighton noted, "but Marjorie is neither an Alice, nor will she be wearing a blue gown."

"I understand your reluctance; however, the only other alternatives were 'Alexander's Ragtime Band,' 'Yoo-Hoo,' and 'You Cannot

Make Your Shimmy Shake on Tea.' Apparently, Mrs. Reynolds is a big fan of dance music," Reverend Price whispered. "She even has sheet music of 'The Charleston.' I'm beginning to suspect she was a flapper back in the day!"

Marjorie and Creighton stared blankly.

"Ehem," Price cleared his throat. "Where was I? Oh, yes, given the choices, I think 'Alice Blue Gown' is the most appropriate selection."

"Don't worry, darling," Creighton soothed. "I'm sure if we take a drive into Hartford, we'll be able to find some shop that has a copy of 'The Wedding March.'"

"You can certainly try," the Reverend encouraged, "but I don't know of too many stores that still carry recordings on cylinder."

"Cylinder?" the couple cried in unison.

"How old is this phonograph?" Creighton asked.

"Oh, I don't know the precise year, but I'm confident it dates from before the war, since I stumbled upon a badly damaged recording of 'Goodbye Broadway, Hello France.'"

"Great," Creighton quipped. "We can save that for the recessional."

"Yes, quite," the minister chuckled. "So, assuming we can't locate a copy of 'The Wedding March' the first few notes of 'Alice Blue Gown' will mark the beginning of the processional. Do you have any bridesmaids?"

Marjorie shook her head. "No, nor flower girls."

"Then it's the maid of honor, Sharon Schutt …"

It was Marjorie's turn to wince. "Reverend? I-I-I-I-I-I don't know about that."

"I'm only quoting Emily. She said you were thinking of asking Sharon Schutt. Didn't make much sense to me either at the time." He drew a line through an entry on his list. "So, we have the maid of honor—whomever that may be—and then," he took a deep breath. "The bride."

At this statement, Marjorie and Creighton exchanged smiles and reached for each other's hands.

Reverend Price continued to expound upon the scene. "When I speak with the couples I've married, none of them ever forget the moment they first laid eyes on each other at their wedding. Women remember the sight of their husbands standing at the altar and men remember the sight of their wives as they entered the church, er, or, in your case, the tent."

"Believe me, Vicar," Creighton started, "those couples might remember gazing into each other's eyes in the church. But for Marjorie and me, this entire experience portends to be unforgettable. Unforgettable from start to finish," he added wearily.

Price beamed. "Good. Your wedding day should be the most memorable day of your life."

"Don't worry," Marjorie quipped, "it will be."

"Oh, I am glad. Most couples would be disappointed to learn that they couldn't be married in the church."

"Disappointed? No," Creighton denied. "We always dreamed of being married beneath a red and white circ-church tent. Everyone has a church wedding nowadays. It's so … so … run of the mill. But a tent wedding is so … so … original. Don't you agree, Marjorie?"

"Hmm? Oh yes. We're quite excited by how … original … our wedding will be. Everyone walks down the aisle to 'The Wedding March,' but it takes a special kind of woman to drag the train of her white satin wedding gown through church fair grounds to the strains of 'Alice Blue Gown.'"

"Just wait. If you're excited now, it gets even better," Price promised.

Marjorie and Creighton nodded and replied in unison, "Ah."

"After the bride's entrance, the ceremony will officially start with the Lord's Prayer. Then I'll say a few words—some remarks about Marjorie, her childhood in Ridgebury followed by some reflections upon Creighton's first appearance in town. After that, there will be a few more prayers, and another song, if we can find one."

"I'm certain we can drum up a copy of 'Happy Days Are Here Again,' or perhaps, 'I Found A Million Dollar Baby,'" Creighton cracked. "For some reason I've always liked that tune. '*It was a lucky April shower* ...'" he sang.

"Yes, and then, after the prayers and the music, there is the exchange of vows and rings." The minister's eyes lit up. "However, it won't end there. In fact, that's where it gets interesting."

"Interesting?" Marjorie and Creighton asked in unison.

"Yes. See, I want the ceremony to be as exciting and mysterious as one of Marjorie's books. So, whereas I'd normally ask, 'If anyone here knows of any reason why these two people should not be joined in holy matrimony,' I'll ask, in its place, 'If anyone here knows who murdered John Braddock, speak now or forever hold your peace.'"

"John Braddock?" they cried in unison.

"Who's John Braddock?" Marjorie quizzed.

"Oh, he's my character. Marjorie, my dear, reading your books has inspired me to take the plunge and write a short mystery story of my own. I haven't had the courage to try and publish it, but I thought it would make a wonderful gift to you and your craft. Keeping in that vein, I thought I'd unveil it at your wedding." He laughed. "Oh, I made a pun. 'Unveil' at a wedding—wedding veil. Too funny."

Creighton smiled politely. "Yes, that's very amusing. Um, Reverend?"

"Yes?"

"When you say you're unveiling your story, do you mean you're reading it aloud?"

"Reading? Heavens no! Acting. You see, when the story opens, the murder has already occurred. In order to reconstruct what has happened to John Braddock, the action rewinds to recount the events of the past forty-eight hours. What occurred to bring about the man's murder? Who had a motive to want him dead?" The minister took a break from his intensity. "What do you think?"

"Very creative," Marjorie praised. "However I'd have to read—"

"I've already approached a few of the ladies with the church league to take on roles," Price interrupted. "My secretary, Mrs. Reynolds has typed up copies of the 'stage version' and Freddie, dear Freddie from the drugstore, has volunteered to make the sets."

"We have sets?" Marjorie asked in disbelief.

"Why of course! This isn't some cheap affair after all," Reverend Price chided. "The wedding of Ridgebury's most esteemed author and the debut of *The Murder of John Braddock* is an event this town will be talking about for some time. It may even make the papers!" He stared into the distance as if the newspaper were posted on the wall across the room. "I can see it now: the first item in the society column or even the local news page—"

"Or the illustrated 'Believe It or Not' feature," Creighton suggested.

"—and the headline will read: 'A Tale of Two Authors: One Weds, the Other . . . the Other . . .' I can't think of anything that rhymes."

". . . Makes Us Scratch Our Heads?" Creighton offered.

The minister nodded approvingly. "Not bad. You might want to try your hand at writing, Creighton."

"Oh no, not me, Vicar. I used to write poetry when I was younger, but then the doctors removed my appendix and I completely lost the ear for rhythm. Now, I'm afraid I can't even tell the difference between iambic pentameter and dactylic hexameter."

Marjorie suppressed a laugh while the minister looked sympathetically at Creighton. "I'm very . . . sorry," Price offered. "That must have been very difficult for you."

"You have no idea. I was once the Limerick King of Coventry, and now . . ." Creighton shook his head mournfully.

"Cheer up, son," the minister advised. "You may not have the ear for poetry, but very soon you'll have a beautiful wife. And you'll marry her in style, to boot! It's all too exciting for words," Reverend Price gushed. "What do you think, Marjorie?"

"For the first time in my life," she stated honestly, "I'm completely and utterly speechless."

After leaving the church rectory, Marjorie and Creighton stopped by Marjorie's cottage so that she could change and prepare for their dinner with Mrs. Patterson. Upon entering the tiny, four-room dwelling, Marjorie removed her shoes and dropped them by the front door.

"A play," she nearly shouted. "Can you believe that our wedding ceremony is going to be topped off with a play?"

Creighton removed his hat and flopped onto the overstuffed living room sofa. "I still can't believe you're walking down the aisle to the sound of 'Alice Blue Gown' being played on a wind-up gramophone. How did they come up with that idea? Were the organ grinder and his monkey too busy that day?"

Marjorie went into the bedroom. "I suppose we should be happy that Mrs. Schutt didn't volunteer to sing."

"Oh, don't worry, darling," Creighton called. "She'll volunteer for something. Remember, we haven't even discussed the reception yet."

Marjorie peeked around the wall dividing the bedroom from the living room. "Oh my goodness! I completely forgot about the reception. I can't imagine what they'll come up with for that!"

"My money's on Mrs. Schutt's Perfection Salad, followed by a round of sandwiches and lemonade—this is the ladies' church league, so no alcohol, remember? Then the wedding cake and—just to provide the appropriate finale to the day—performances by a conjurer and a barber shop quartet."

"Well, my question is," she called from the bedroom, "if we're not using the church for the wedding, can we use the parish hall for the reception?"

Marjorie's cat, Sam, leapt onto the cushion beside Creighton. The Englishman raised a hand to pet the animal, but was met with a loud hiss, followed by the swat of a furry paw. "Why bother?" he sighed. "I say we hold the reception under the Big Top. It evokes the theme of the whole event: a circus, minus the elephants."

Marjorie's laughter rang out from the other room. "Or clowns. We don't have those either."

"I'd have to disagree with you there, darling," Creighton argued. "If anything, we have too many clowns."

Marjorie emerged from the bedroom, resplendent in a light-blue chiffon evening gown. Around her neck hung the diamond filigree necklace Creighton had let her "borrow" during their first case.

"Look at you!" Creighton rose from his spot on the sofa, allowing his hat to drop onto the cushion behind him. Sam immediately seized the opportunity to sit upon the warm object.

Marjorie twirled about to show off the backless design of her gown. "Like?"

"Like? You look so good, we might not make it back to my house." He took her face in his hands and kissed her.

"But Mrs. Patterson would be very disappointed," she reminded. "And Agnes has probably been cooking all day."

"Hmm," he grunted in acceptance. "You are a clever one, aren't you? Well, you've managed to escape this time, but I want a rain check."

"You've got one, Mr. Ashcroft," she smiled.

"Good, then let's go pick up Mrs. P. and get this show on the road."

"Speaking of Mrs. Patterson," Marjorie mentioned, "do you think we should talk to her about our concerns regarding the ceremony?"

Creighton drew a deep breath. "I don't know. She means well and I'd hate to hurt her feelings. But, I do think we should make it clear that we want a less ... dramatic wedding than she and the townsfolk have planned for us. If we phrase it the right way, I'm sure she'll understand. All Mrs. P. wants is for us to get married and be happy."

"You're right, she does," Marjorie agreed. "As much as she enjoys the wedding planning, I'm sure she wouldn't want us to participate in something that makes us unhappy."

"Of course. Although, with everything we've heard about the plans, I'm looking forward to the wedding."

Marjorie was incredulous. "You are?"

"Yes. I don't know why. Possibly it's the same macabre instinct that makes us stop and gawk at automobile accidents or listen to Father Coughlin on the wireless, but I would like to see what transpires. I'd prefer it if I were a spectator and it was someone else's wedding that was being commandeered, but on a human interest level, this should be quite amusing."

"If we survive the experience," she added.

"Yes, that's always an issue, isn't it? However, for now, we'll pick up Mrs. P., go to Kensington House, have a few drinks, then dinner, and let the subject of the wedding introduce itself. This is, after all, supposed to be her evening." He kissed Marjorie on the forehead and reached over the back of the sofa for his hat. His hand grabbed hold of something furry.

He cursed the feline under his breath and pulled the hat from under Sam's hindquarters. "Talking to Mrs. P. about the wedding will be a cinch," he stated as he tried to bring his hat back to life. "Living with this creature from hell after we're married, however, will not."

NINETEEN

Creighton, dressed in an elegant black dinner jacket, placed three crystal martini glasses along the edge of the ornately carved walnut bar. "My dear Mrs. P., you're in for a rare treat: the Ashcroft Martini."

A girlish giggle arose from Mrs. Patterson's spot on the Biedermeier sofa. "Oh how you kids do spoil me! First inviting me for dinner and now introducing me to exotic drinks. Do you know I've never actually had a martini before?" She giggled again. "It sounds so very decadent!"

"I don't know if I'd call it decadent," Marjorie called from the dining room, where she was in the process of setting the table. "But even if it were, I can't think of anyone worthier of indulging than you. You do so much for everyone, it's high time you received some pampering."

Creighton poured a splash of vermouth in each glass. "I second that notion," he cheered. "And if you think you're being spoiled now, just wait until dinner. Agnes is whipping up her famous—"

Creighton's recitation of the evening's menu was interrupted by the sound of the doorbell.

Arthur appeared in the living room doorway with Detective Jameson in tow. "Detective Jameson," the butler announced his guest.

"Jameson!" Creighton hailed. "How are you?"

"Hi Creighton, sorry to barge in," the detective apologized.

"It's no imposition." He retrieved a fourth glass from the bottom of the bar and gestured to the elderly lady on the sofa. "Marjorie and Mrs. P. were just joining me for dinner and drinks."

Jameson removed his hat and greeted the elderly woman. "Mrs. Patterson, how are you?"

"Very well, Detective. Very well indeed. How have you been since I last saw you?"

"Oh, you know the routine. Work, home, work. Same old, same old."

"How's the murder case going?" she inquired

Marjorie entered from the adjacent dining room, her eyes wide in astonishment. "Murder case? You mean you know that Creighton and I aren't investigating a missing person's case?"

Mrs. Patterson waved her hand. "Of course I do! Not only was the 'mu-kidnapping' conversation a dead giveaway, but you get that gleam in your eye whenever there's a dead body around. It's rather obvious."

Marjorie looked to Creighton for confirmation. "Is she right? Do I get a gleam in my eye?"

"Your eyes do get a trifle googly, darling," the Englishman told her.

"Now, Detective," Mrs. Patterson continued, "tell us why you've come, before Marjorie makes such a sulky face that she completely swallows her bottom lip."

Creighton stifled a laugh while Marjorie made a conscious effort to thrust her bottom lip forward.

Jameson was thrown momentarily off kilter. "Yes, ma'am. I was, uh, driving past Kensington House on my way to dinner when I saw the lights on. I was going to call later from Sharon's house, but I figured I'd stop by and let you know I ordered the exhumation of Cynthia Taylor's body. They should be able to get to the autopsy by tomorrow afternoon."

"It seems macabre to say it, but that's excellent news," Marjorie stated.

"If we knew for a fact that Ronnie Carter's allegations against Trent Taylor were true, it would enable us to see things in a whole new light." Creighton poured chilled gin into one of the glasses, topped it with an olive, and handed it to Mrs. Patterson. "Here you go, Mrs. P. Let me know how this tickles your fancy."

"It doesn't matter whether the allegations were true or not," Marjorie instructed. "The mere fact that Ronnie made them in the first place gives Trent Taylor a strong motive for wanting her out of the way. The only thing the autopsy will prove is whether or not Trent has killed before. If he has, it makes him a more likely suspect than Michael Barnwell."

"More likely than Barnwell?" Robert challenged.

"Yes," Marjorie averred. "Once you've crossed that boundary to committing murder, it's much easier to do so again."

"Granted," the detective agreed. "But what about the suitcase beneath Michael Barnwell's desk? How do you account for that?"

"That's simple," Marjorie pooh-poohed. "Helen was on break."

"Huh?"

Marjorie sighed noisily. "Helen. The receptionist at New England Allied. You witnessed today what happens when Helen goes on break. If she were away from her desk, it would have been very easy for someone—anyone—to sneak in, plant the case, and leave."

Creighton approached with two martinis. He handed one to Marjorie and the other to Jameson. "No thanks," the detective refused. "I'm on my way to the Schutts for dinner."

"Again?" Marjorie said in surprise. "Weren't you just there last night?"

"Really?" Creighton feigned innocence. "You've been to the Schutts for dinner that frequently? I had no idea you were seeing Sharon."

"I'm not," Jameson asserted.

"That's not what Louise Schutt's been saying," Mrs. Patterson spoke up.

"She's been telling everyone who'll listen that you threw me over for Sharon," Marjorie recounted.

"She is? Where on earth would she have gotten that idea?" Jameson asked in disbelief.

"You know the Schutts. Where do they get any of their ideas?" Creighton gave an overly loud chuckle.

"Are you sure you aren't seeing Sharon?" Mrs. Patterson checked.

"No," Jameson maintained. "At least I don't think I am. We never spend any time alone. It's always dinner with her folks, followed by *Fibber McGee and Molly*, then dessert—if I'm lucky, it's rhubarb pie—and a round of tiddlywinks."

"You play tiddlywinks?" Marjorie asked in astonishment.

"I not only play tiddlywinks, I'm quite good at it. I've dethroned Mr. Schutt as champion." He stuck his chest out proudly.

"Do you know, in all the times I ate dinner there, the Schutts never invited me to play tiddlywinks?" Creighton said wistfully. "I must say I'm jealous, Jameson."

"I guess they just like me better than they liked you," Jameson taunted.

"You're right, they probably do. And I suppose I'll have to live with that knowledge ... somehow."

Marjorie jabbed the facetious Creighton in the ribs with her elbow. "What time are the Schutts expecting you?" she inquired sweetly.

"Around six, I think."

Marjorie glanced at the clock on the mantle. "Around six? If I know the Schutts, that means six on the dot and it's already six thirty. Maybe you should call and tell them you're running late."

With that, the doorbell rang.

"Uh-oh," the foursome exclaimed in unison.

Several seconds elapsed before Arthur appeared in the doorway to introduce the latest arrival, but the thin, reedy voice originating from the front door and echoing down the foyer to the living room rendered all introductions unnecessary.

"Robert!" Sharon squealed as she caught sight of the latest in the long line of Schutt victims. "I've been looking all over for you! You had me so worried. Mother planned supper for six o'clock."

Creighton was about to slink out of sight when Jameson stopped him, grabbed the martini from his hand and drank it down in one gulp. "Sorry I kept you waiting, but I had some business to discuss with Creighton and Marjorie. Oh, and Mrs. Patterson too."

The elderly woman waved a friendly hello, her cheeks flushed pink from the alcohol of the martini.

Sharon whirled around in surprise. So fixated had she been on her prey, that she had failed to notice the presence of anyone else in the room. "Hello, Mrs. Patterson. Hello, Creighton" she tittered. When she caught a glimpse of Marjorie the smile ran away from her face. "Hello, Marjorie."

"Hello, Sharon," the writer replied with equal iciness.

Meanwhile, Creighton, tinged with guilt for having sicced Sharon upon the detective in the first place, tried a diversionary tactic. "Sharon, how about a cocktail before you go back home?" He pulled a fifth martini glass from the bar.

"Oh, I don't drink, Creighton," Sharon whined. "Mother says that's for 'fast' women." She eyed Marjorie, who countered the glare by biting into her martini olive with a snarl.

Creighton returned the fifth glass to the cabinet. "How about dinner, then? There's more than enough for everyone and your mother's meal is probably more well-done than usual by now." He punctuated the statement with a dazzling smile.

"Oh no, we couldn't. We ... what are you having?"

"Martinis to start with, and then Agnes is whipping up her famous—"

"Sharon!" The booming voice of Louise Schutt drowned out all other sound in the room.

Arthur, dwarfed by Louise's intimidating heft, apologized meekly. "She didn't ring the bell, sir. She let herself in. I tried to stop her but it was no use ..."

"That's fine, Arthur," Creighton excused. "I didn't fancy driving you to Hartford Hospital this evening anyway."

"Yes, sir." Arthur made his way back into the kitchen.

"Sharon," Mrs. Schutt exclaimed. "What do you think you're doing here in this house with—with—alcohol?" Louise continued her temperance tirade. "Come along home. I have the chicken keeping warm."

"Yes, mother," Sharon answered obediently.

"You as well, Detective Jameson," Louise ordered.

Jameson hemmed and hawed. "Well, I—if it's all right with you, Mrs. Schutt, I'd much rather—"

"I made rhubarb pie," she said enticingly.

"Coming, Mrs. Schutt," the detective replied without missing a beat. He followed Sharon out of the living room obediently. "Bet I can beat your dad at tiddlywinks again," he taunted.

"Bet you can't," Sharon dared as they made their exit.

Mrs. Schutt watched her youngest offspring and smiled triumphantly. "Good evening, Mr. Ashcroft. Good evening, Marjorie." On her way out, she noticed Mrs. Patterson seated on the sofa, an empty martini glass in hand. "Emily Patterson!" she exclaimed. "Have you been drinking?"

"Yes, I have," the other woman proudly announced. "I just had my first martini, and now I'm going to have another." She held the glass up for a refill. "Creighton?"

Creighton retrieved the glass with a wink. "Right away, Mrs. P."

Louise's mouth assumed a myriad of shapes, as it strove desperately to formulate the word that would adequately express her indignation. In the end, all she could say is "Well!" before stomping her way through the foyer and out the front door.

Creighton retrieved Marjorie's glass and set it between Mrs. Patterson's glass and the clean glass he had designated for himself. "Ah, peace and quiet at last!"

Marjorie sat beside Mrs. Patterson on the Biedermeier sofa. "Oh! I thought they'd never leave. And then you went ahead and invited them for dinner. I don't know why you'd do such a thing, Creighton. What's gotten into you lately?"

"Just being nice, darling. I feel for Jameson. Remember, I was once a passenger on that runaway train." He shook a chrome shaker filled with ice and gin and emptied the contents into the three vermouth-coated glasses. "Now, however, I'm here with two beautiful women and three perfect martinis—"

The doorbell rang again.

"Four perfect martinis," he amended as he grabbed another glass from beneath the bar.

Arthur appeared in the living room doorway with a stocky, ruddy-faced man with light-colored hair. "Officer Patrick Noonan," he announced.

"I never thought I'd say this, Noonan, but I'm actually relieved to see you," Creighton welcomed.

Noonan removed his hat. "Huh?"

Marjorie rose from the sofa and retrieved a martini for herself and Mrs. Patterson. "We thought you were one of the Schutts," she explained. "Louise was just here to collect Sharon, and unfortunately Robert, for dinner. They left a few moments ago."

"Jameson and Sharon, huh? That's still going on, then?" Noonan laughed. "Jameson don't like talking about it, so I don't ask him anymore."

"You're a very wise man," Mrs. Patterson remarked.

“Hiya, Mrs. Patterson. I didn’t see you there. How ya doin’?”

“Fine. Just fine.” She raised her glass. “Martini?”

“Don’t know. Never had one.”

“Oh, they’re good,” she vouched. “Try one.”

Noonan shrugged. “Why not? I’m Irish and I’m off-duty.”

“One martini, it is,” Creighton declared. “On second thought, there’s four of us, maybe I should use a pitcher.” He retrieved a glass pitcher from beneath the bar and went about his work.

“What brings you here this evening, Officer Noonan?” Marjorie asked.

Noonan placed his hat on the coffee table and sat down beside Mrs. Patterson. “I was looking for Detective Jameson. I wanted to tell him that Heller wasn’t able to lift the prints from that suitcase. He tried, but no luck.”

“Anything else?”

“Nope, that’s about it.”

Creighton handed him a full martini glass and placed the pitcher on the coffee table. “You came all this way to tell him that? I thought you’d be home with the wife and kids by now.”

Noonan took a sip of martini and, finding it palatable, belted back the remainder of the glass. “My wife’s visiting her sister in Elmira. Took the kids with her.” He crunched on his olive morosely.

“You mean you’re all alone? You poor thing! You should have dinner with us,” Marjorie invited.

“Yes,” Creighton chimed in. “That’s an excellent idea. No need to go home to an empty house when we have plenty of food here.”

Noonan's eyes grew misty. "Gee, that's sportin' of you, Creighton. Really sportin'. It is kinda lonely at home. It just ain't the same without Eileen and the kids."

"Of course it isn't," Mrs. Patterson soothed.

The doorbell rang a fourth time.

"Well, rest easy, Noonan," Creighton assured the officer. "If there's one thing Kensington House isn't, it's lonely."

Arthur appeared in the doorway with a familiar redheaded man trailing behind him. "Mr. Trent Taylor." The butler looked the mechanic up and down before returning to his post.

"Mr. Taylor," Creighton greeted. "May I offer you a—" he lifted the now empty pitcher from the coffee table. "Drink?"

"Yeah, that'd be great." Taylor swaggered into the living room. "Quite a place you've got here, Mr. Ashcroft. You have a definite eye for beauty." He surveyed the surroundings, including Marjorie, with appraising steel blue eyes. "Hello. Miss McCarthy, right?"

"Miss McClelland," Marjorie corrected. "Soon to be Mrs. Ashcroft."

"Engaged, huh? I was right, Mr. Ashcroft. You do have an eye for beauty."

"Is there a reason for you being here, Mr. Taylor?" Mrs. Patterson asked in the sternest tone she could muster.

"Who are you?" Taylor demanded.

Noonan took Marjorie by the arm and pulled her onto the settee, nestling her protectively between himself and Mrs. Patterson. "She's Marjorie's mother," the officer replied glibly.

"And he's Marjorie's father," Creighton rejoined over Trent's shoulder. He handed the mechanic his martini. "Cheers. Although it appears this isn't your first beverage this evening. So why don't you just finish your drink, say what you want to say, and get out of here?"

"Whoa, settle down there," Taylor laughed. "Look, I'm not here to start anything with you. I admire your fiancée because she's a good-looking woman. There's nothing wrong with that. But I'm not looking to make trouble. I've had to deal with troublemakers myself these past few months. Or should I say one troublemaker in particular?"

"Veronica Carter?" Marjorie deduced.

"You said it. Ever since I told her I wanted to call it quits, she was out to make my life miserable. All I want to do is run my shop and live my life. That's all. I was a devoted husband to Cynthia until my foot slipped once. Once! And I've been paying for it ever since."

"Paying how? Because your claim was denied? Or is there something more?" Marjorie asked for clarification.

"The claim was part of it, and that's the part I could have lived with just fine. The money would have been nice, but it can't replace Cynthia."

"You're making me cry over here," Noonan said sarcastically. "Hurry it up, will ya?"

Taylor's grip on the martini glass tightened. "Okay, I'll cut to the chase. Today, I got word that my wife's body is being dug up. It's bad enough that she had doctors poking and prodding her when she was alive, but now they're going to take her out of the ground and start ripping apart her bones because some brazen hussy says I poisoned her!" He flung his glass against the fireplace, causing it to explode into tiny shards.

Marjorie and Mrs. Patterson clung to each other while Noonan arched forward and reached for his gun.

"The cheap tart's dead, and she's still hell bent on destroying my life," Taylor ranted. "God, I hate her! When I found out she was dead I was relieved. I was relieved because she couldn't hurt me any more. But here she is making a mess for me again. And you two"—he glared at Marjorie and Creighton in turn—"are helping her do it. Why can't you let things be? Ronnie's dead and whoever killed her did the world a service! Why can't you leave it at that and go on with your lives?" He began to sob uncontrollably. "Why can't you leave me alone? Why can't you leave Cynthia alone? Why can't you just let her rest in peace?"

The doorbell rang.

Arthur appeared in the doorway. "It's a lady, sir. She wishes to see you and Miss McClelland alone, in the foyer."

"I'll stay here with Taylor," Noonan offered. "He won't pull anything funny on my watch."

"Thanks, Noonan," Creighton said gratefully. "I'm glad you happened by tonight. Don't go anywhere, eh?"

"What? And miss this?" Noonan chuckled. "Nah, I'm here as long as you and Miss McClelland need me. If this is the hurly durve, I can't wait to see what you two are cooking up for a main course."

"You and me both, Noonan," the Englishman acknowledged before following his fiancée into the foyer.

"Elizabeth," Marjorie asked as she approached the figure standing in the front door, "is everything okay?"

Elizabeth Barnwell was dressed in a black dress and a black cloche hat with veil. A groggy Michael Jr. rested his head against her bosom. “Oh, everything’s fine, Miss McClelland. I just stopped by to tell you and Mr. Ashcroft that I’m spending the weekend with my parents. The past few weeks have been so upsetting that my mother has offered to take care of little Michael while I get some rest. And my father’s going to help me with some of the bills. Michael’s been gone less than a week and there’s already a bunch of things due next week. I—I—I never wrote out a check before. My mother always told me that was a man’s job. Handling money, I mean.”

“Does your husband know you’re going?” Marjorie asked.

“Yes, I saw him today. It’s terrible, him being in jail, but at least I’m able to see him. I spent the past few days thinking he was dead—you can’t imagine what a relief it is to know he’s alive. Of course, it would be nicer if he were home and not facing murder charges, but right now I need to rest and regain my strength.”

“Good move,” Creighton approved. “There’s bound to be a long road ahead. For all of you.” He tousled Michael Jr.’s hair.

Marjorie, in the meantime, had skipped ahead to the task of gathering essential information. “What’s your parents’ number, Elizabeth? Just in case we need to reach you.”

“I already anticipated that question.” Elizabeth handed them a slip of paper bearing a telephone number written in large, childish numerals. “There it is. Call any time you like.”

“You don’t have to leave right now, do you?” Creighton queried. “We haven’t eaten dinner yet, and I’m sure you haven’t either—if you’ve been eating anything at all lately. Why don’t you stay a bit? It will do you some good. Put Michael Jr. down in one of the guest rooms and join us for a drink and dinner. We have plenty of food and a pitcher of martinis big enough for six—um, four…" He counted on one hand. "Five. We have enough for all five of us."

"That's very kind of you, Mr. Ashcroft, but I have a taxi waiting." She gestured outside. "We'll be back Monday, but if you need to reach me before then, just give me a call. There's not much to do in my hometown, so odds are someone will be around to answer."

Elizabeth gave Marjorie a hug and Creighton a kiss on the cheek. "Thank you for the invitation. Thank you…for everything," she bade before heading off into the gathering darkness.

Creighton closed the door slowly behind her, only to feel a tap on his shoulder. "Hey, let me through!" a boisterous Trent Taylor demanded.

Noonan called from the living room, "It's okay. He's on the level. I convinced him to go home and sleep it off."

Creighton opened the door wide and saluted. "Then, by all means, Mr. Taylor. Don't let me keep you." He slammed the door as soon as Taylor cleared the threshold.

Marjorie was wide-eyed with excitement. "What do you think of that? You saw that temper of his! Do you think Trent Taylor could be our killer?"

"Don't know. Don't care. I'm through discussing the case this evening. Tonight it's all about you and me." He slung a careless arm around Marjorie's shoulders and escorted her back to the living room.

They walked in on a heated debate between Mrs. Patterson and Officer Noonan.

"Yes, I know there are some funny lines," Mrs. Patterson was saying in her sweet, high-pitched voice, "yet I can't help but find *Fibber McGee and Molly* farfetched. All the action takes place in their living room—people coming and going and coming and going. I don't know of anyone who has so many visitors in one night!"

Marjorie and Creighton looked at each other but declined comment.

"How about another round?" Creighton asked of Marjorie.

"Another?" she exclaimed. "You and I haven't even finished the first one yet."

"You know, you're right. We should remedy that!"

Creighton was in the process of chipping ice and swirling vermouth, when the doorbell rang yet again. In frustration, he stepped away from the bar and plopped the bottle of vermouth, the bowl of olives, and the bottle of gin on the coffee table. "Here. I'm not mixing anything else tonight. I leave you all to your own devices."

"It's another woman, Mr. Ashcroft," Arthur informed his employer from the doorway of the living room. "She doesn't look well. Not well at all. I think you should come at once."

Creighton and Marjorie wasted no time in following him out of the living room, through the foyer, and to the front door.

Once there, they found Diana Hoffman standing at the threshold, paralyzed. The blood had drained from her face, making her fair skin appear almost translucent in the light of the foyer chandelier.

"Diana!" Marjorie called as she rushed forward and took the young woman's hands in her own. "Creighton, darling, she's freezing! It's as if she's experienced a dreadful shock. Talk to us, dear," she coaxed. "Tell us what's wrong."

"I... I think I've made a mistake coming here. A terrible mistake."

"What do you mean, 'a mistake'?" Creighton urged. "Miss Hoffman, we're here. You're safe. Tell us about the mistake you made."

"No, I need to—I need to see someone first. And I need some time to think."

A silhouette approached the front of the house, growing larger and larger until it overtook Diana Hoffman and pushed her against the door frame. It was an agitated Gordon Merchant.

"I knew I should have had that revolving door installed," Creighton quipped.

"Elizabeth? Where is she?" Gordon Merchant demanded. "Are she and the baby okay?"

"Yes, they're fine. Now please calm down, Mr. Merchant!" Marjorie scolded. "You're crushing Miss Hoffman."

"Sorry, miss," he apologized to the blonde woman in the pale turquoise dress.

"It's all right," Diana muttered. "I was just leaving." She turned on one heel and hurried down the walkway.

"Diana, don't leave," Marjorie pleaded as she took off after her.

Meanwhile, Gordon spilled his tale of woe to Creighton. "I'm sorry for intruding like I did, but I was hoping Elizabeth might still be here. I followed her here, you see."

"Followed?"

"Yes, I went over to the house to see if she and little Michael needed anything. When I got there, she was leaving. She had Michael in her arms and was getting into a cab. I thought perhaps she was going out for the evening, but then I saw the driver loading a suitcase into the trunk. I waved, in hopes that maybe she'd stop and tell me where she was going, but she didn't even notice. She didn't even look at me."

"She's going through a difficult time, Gordon," Creighton explained delicately. "She may know you and like you, but she just found out her husband was having an affair and may have murdered his mistress. She's probably having a hard time trusting anyone right now, let alone a friend of her husband's. Even if that friend is you."

This seemed to satisfy the blonde man.

"If I were you, I'd go home and get some sleep. Elizabeth will be back on Monday. Try talking to her then," Creighton advised.

"You're right, Mr. Ashcroft, she is under a lot of strain, what with the baby and Mike in jail, and her being all alone. It must be tough," Gordon agreed. "I'll do what you said. I'll give her some time. I'll wait until Monday. But if I need to talk to someone before then, can I call you?"

"Of course, now get going."

"Thanks, Mr. Ashcroft!" Gordon called as he disappeared into the gathering darkness.

When Merchant was out of sight, Creighton called out the front door, "Marjorie."

There was no reply.

"Marjorie?" he called again, this time questioning.

His call was not met by a feminine voice, but was instead answered by a series of gunshots ripping through the warm summer air.

TWENTY

"Hold tight! Don't move!" Noonan yelled as he bounded out the door and down the walkway, his police-issued revolver at the ready.

From this distance, in the dwindling twilight, Creighton was able to pick out what resembled two heaps of crumpled blue fabric: one lying at the bottom of the slate walk, the other a few feet away, at the edge of the circular gravel driveway.

Roused by the gunshots, Mrs. Patterson had vacated her seat in the living room and joined Creighton in the doorway. "Marjorie!" she gasped.

Noonan surveyed the area and signaled the all clear.

"Wait here, Mrs. P.," Creighton instructed before taking off like a shot toward the nearest blue-clad figure. "Marjorie!" He knelt beside her. "Marjorie?"

"Hmmm?" she replied groggily as she endeavored to rise from her prone position.

"Shh," Creighton cautioned. "Take it easy, darling. Move slowly."

Marjorie sat upright on the slate and held her head. A trickle of blood ran from her left temple and down her cheek.

"Darling, you're hurt!" Creighton exclaimed in concern.

"No, no … I'm okay. The bullet just grazed me. I heard it whiz past my ear." She turned to where the other woman had been standing just a few seconds earlier

"How's Diana?" she asked.

Noonan shook his head grimly. "She's dead."

Marjorie sat on the Biedermeier settee while Dr. Heller cleaned her wound and dressed it with a clean bandage.

"You're a very lucky young woman," Heller observed. "A half-inch more to the left and you'd be on a slab next to Miss Hoffman."

"I'm sure they're all the rage at cocktail parties, Doctor," she answered facetiously, "but would you mind keeping the morgue jokes to a minimum? I'm funny that way."

Heller smiled. "Just stating the facts as they are, Miss McClelland. You've had a close call."

"Hmph," Mrs. Patterson remarked. "And she tried to pass this whole thing off as a 'simple' kidnapping case."

Noonan looked at the older woman. "Kidnapping? This isn't a kidnapping, this is murder! What did she say she and Creighton found in the cellar of that house? A canned ham?"

Heller approached Creighton. "I'm going to give Marjorie some pills to keep on hand. Just in case she has trouble sleeping."

"Good. Marjorie's a brave girl, but it catches up with her sometimes." He listened as Noonan and Patterson exchanged comments, neither understanding what the other was saying. "You wouldn't happen to have a few extra for me, would you, Doctor?"

The doorbell rang.

Jameson entered. "Sorry I missed all the action. I came as soon as I could."

"That's all right, Jameson," Creighton ribbed good-naturedly. "We all know how riveting those last few winks can be."

The detective ignored the Englishman's jibes. "What happened?"

Creighton sat beside Marjorie on the settee. "Diana Hoffman's been murdered," he informed the detective. "Shot in the head right outside my front door. Lunatic almost got Marjorie too."

"Are you all right?" Jameson inquired of Marjorie.

"I'm fine," she assured. "Thanks."

"Did you happen to get a good look at the guy?" Jameson pressed.

She shook her head. "No. All I can tell you for certain is that Diana had come here for a reason—I don't know what that reason was, but she was upset. Visibly upset and shaken. She ran out of here, suddenly, and I ran after her. Before I knew exactly what was happening, I heard the shots, felt something graze the side of my head, and I fell to the ground. I must have hit my head on the slate and must have been knocked unconscious, because that's the last I remember until Creighton came and got me."

"Any idea who might have done it?" Jameson inquired.

"Who couldn't have done it?" Noonan scoffed. "The place was a free-for-all."

Mrs. Patterson concurred. "Officer Noonan's right. It's been one person after another all evening."

"Tell me the order in which they arrived," Jameson instructed.

"Trent Taylor was the first," Creighton explained. "He was fired up, partly because of his wife's disinterment and partly because of booze."

"Partly?" Noonan heckled. "The guy was gassed and looking for a good brawl. He was so fired up, he threw a glass against the fireplace."

"Interesting," Jameson mused. "Who next?"

"Elizabeth Barnwell," Creighton stated. "She stopped by to let us know she's going to her parents' place for the weekend. Elizabeth never came into the house—she stood in the foyer while Trent was in the living room."

"Who left first?"

"Elizabeth," Marjorie recalled. "Trent left immediately after she did."

"And then?" Jameson prodded.

"Diana Hoffman," Creighton recounted. "Followed closely by Gordon Merchant. Gordon literally bumped into Diana as she stood in our doorway. His knickers were in a twist because Elizabeth Barnwell snubbed him. He trailed her cab here in hopes of catching up with her. I convinced him to go home and await her return Monday morning. He followed my advice and left. That's when we heard the gunshots."

"And none of you saw anyone?" he verified.

"Not a soul," Noonan asserted.

"So what are we left with?" Jameson asked.

"Roast beef and Yorkshire pudding," Agnes announced as she carted a large silver tray into the dining room. "Potatoes, green beans, and horseradish cream are coming up. I know it's been a hectic night, so I'll put everything on the buffet. This way you can eat whenever, and wherever, you like."

"Thank you, Agnes," Creighton said gratefully. "You're one in a million. Don't worry about cleaning up tonight. I'll get it. It's been a long day for you."

"Thank you, sir. And how are you feeling, Miss McClelland? Arthur and I were dreadful worried about you."

"I'm fine, Agnes," Marjorie responded. "You're very sweet for asking. Thank Arthur for me too."

Once the side dishes were in place, Agnes made her leave and the ravenous sextet filled their plates to enjoy them, buffet style, in the living room.

Several minutes elapsed before anyone spoke.

"So what are we left with?" Jameson asked, between bites.

"Two dead women, four suspects, one bloodstained suitcase, and a grazed ear," Marjorie summarized.

"It doesn't make sense to me," Jameson thought aloud. "Who would have wanted Diana Hoffman dead?"

"Without understanding the cause of her emotional upset, there's no way to know," Marjorie asserted. "But it's obvious she either knew or had just discovered something about Ronnie's murder. Something that might have helped us find the killer."

"That's just speculation," Jameson argued. "We have no evidence apart from what she said when she came here, which was what exactly?"

"She said she had made a mistake coming here. When we pressed her to tell us about the mistake, she said she needed to see someone first. She said she needed to think." Marjorie shrugged. "I can only assume that she was going to tell us something and then thought better of it—like she needed to think because she was uncertain about something. Still, it doesn't explain her physical state. Her face was pale and she was shivering. As if she was frightened of something, or someone."

"Trent Taylor left before she did," Creighton offered. "What if he had been lurking about the grounds and Diana saw him on her way in. She and he used to be an item, but it's been a little while since they've seen each other. That might have shaken her up a bit."

"It could have," Marjorie conceded, "but being upset over an old flame wouldn't have gotten her killed. No, I think we need to look at each suspect individually. First, we have Trent Taylor."

"My bet's on him," Noonan interjected. "What about you, Emmy?" he asked Mrs. Patterson.

"I'm with you, Patrick," the elderly woman agreed. "He had a vile temper."

Creighton raised a questioning eyebrow. "Emmy?"

"Trent Taylor had a strong motive for wanting Veronica Carter dead," Marjorie continued. "The story about Trent having poisoned his wife has caused him insurmountable problems: denial of his insurance claim, possible arrest, and now the exhumation of his wife's body."

Creighton nodded. "He said right here, in this very room, that he hated her."

"And Diana might have needed time to consider giving Trent the opportunity to explain the evidence she found, rather than handing it over to us or the police," Marjorie pointed out. "Especially if Diana still harbored some romantic feelings for him."

"I hadn't even thought about that," Jameson admitted.

"Speaking of romantic feelings, that brings us to Gordon Merchant." Marjorie moved the conversation forward to the next suspect. "Gordon Merchant is an interesting suspect because, out of everyone, he had the best opportunity to murder Veronica Carter and then frame Michael Barnwell for the crime. Motive? He's in love with Elizabeth Barnwell and he knew about Michael's affair with Veronica. If he hated Michael for being married to Elizabeth, he hated him even more for betraying her. It would have been easy for him to kill Veronica and then plant the suitcase under Michael's desk. And doing so would have sent Michael to prison, thus clearing the way for him and Elizabeth."

"Also, his story about how Michael and Veronica met is quite different from Michael Barnwell's," Creighton interjected. "He might have lied in order to cast even more suspicion in Barnwell's direction."

"The question is," Marjorie stated, "how desperate of a man is he?"

"Very—if his performance this evening is any indication," Creighton opined.

"And then there's Elizabeth Barnwell—"

"Elizabeth?" Jameson questioned. "You don't actually think she's wrapped up in this, do you?"

"No, but I have to include her. She had as good a motive as anyone for wanting Veronica Carter dead," Marjorie highlighted. "She could easily have murdered her and pinned everything on Michael. Remember, she got us involved in this case. And we have only her word that the key and address were in her husband's pocket. We don't know how far she'd go to take revenge for her husband's betrayal."

"Speaking of betrayal, even Diana Hoffman had a good reason to kill Veronica Carter," Creighton chimed in. "Assuming, in fact, that Ronnie stole Trent Taylor away from her."

"The problem with that theory," Noonan was quick to mention, "is that Diana Hoffman is dead. She didn't come all this way to shoot herself in your driveway. I say we cross her off the list. Also off the list is Michael Barnwell. He couldn't have shot Diana because he's in the stir."

"Not to make your unenviable task more difficult," Heller interjected, "but from a medical perspective, there could indeed be two killers. The modus operandi of the second murder doesn't match the first. One victim was beaten—a brutal, messy, hands-on sort of crime. The second was shot—a slightly cleaner, somewhat detached method of killing someone."

"Great," Noonan commented. "Just when I thought we were getting somewhere in this case, now there may be two nuts on the loose!"

"Let's not get carried away here," Jameson spoke up. "The problem with all these theories—be there one murderer, two murderers, or an entire army—is that Diana Hoffman is dead. We can find a reason for each of our suspects to want to kill Veronica Carter, but Diana's death just doesn't seem to fit, unless..."

"Unless she knew something about Veronica's murder," Marjorie asserted as she took a bite of Yorkshire pudding.

"There's that, yes, but there's also another possibility: Diana Hoffman might not have been the intended victim."

The room fell silent.

Jameson expounded upon his theory. "When I got here, the medics were taking Diana Hoffman away. I couldn't help but notice that she was wearing a light blue dress and that she, like you, Marjorie, had blonde hair. A different shade, perhaps, but outdoors, in the twilight, it would have been very difficult to tell the two of you apart."

"You're saying that the shooter might have been after Marjorie," Creighton surmised.

Marjorie moved to the edge of her seat. "Me? But why would anyone want to shoot me?"

"Need I point out, darling, that this isn't the first time someone's taken a shot at you?" Creighton explained delicately. "Although most of us here find you quite lovable, when you spend your time nosing about murders, you're bound to rub someone the wrong way. Just look at Trent Taylor, for instance. He was more than a bit miffed at you for having his wife's body being exhumed."

"He was 'miffed' at both of us," she corrected. "However, I was the only one who got shot. I'm always the one who gets shot. Why doesn't anyone ever shoot you? After all, you 'nose about in murders' just as much as I do."

He shrugged. "I'm simply too good-looking to be mistaken as someone else, and I'm just entirely too likable to be bumped off."

"Ugh," Marjorie rolled her eyes.

"Enough joking, darling," Creighton's voice took a serious tone. "You and Diana weren't very far apart when we found you. And from far away, you did resemble each other: blonde hair, blue dresses. Yours is an evening gown and Diana's was a daytime dress, but I don't think a shooter would take much notice of hemlines, especially if you were both running."

"We were moving quickly," Marjorie acknowledge. "And what with the poor light and the shadows, I suppose it's possible." Still, she was not entirely convinced.

"Reminds me of that song," Heller thought aloud. "How does it go again? '*Shadows on the wall... I can see them fall... Two silhouettes in blue... Here I am, but where are you?*'"

TWENTY-ONE

Marjorie, dressed in a nightgown, a lightweight robe, and a pair of slippers, made her way downstairs from one of the Kensington House guest rooms to the lower-level kitchen.

"Good morning, Marjorie," Mrs. Patterson greeted.

Creighton stood at the counter, sliding a portion of scrambled eggs from a cast-iron skillet onto a large white plate. "Good morning, darling. How did you sleep?"

"All right," she replied with a yawn.

"I know Kensington House isn't quite your home yet, and you probably missed being in a more ... familiar ... bed last night," he said with a mischievous twinkle in his eye that made Marjorie blush. "But I felt a lot better knowing you and Mrs. Patterson were here where I could keep an eye on both of you. Call me overprotective, but I would have been camped out on the Ridgebury village green all night long, watching your front doors for intruders." He bestowed Marjorie with a tender kiss before garnishing the dish with two strips of bacon and a slice of toast. He deposited the whole thing in front of Mrs. Patterson, who was seated at the head of a long wooden table.

"I gave Agnes and Arthur time off for good behavior," Creighton explained. "Agnes, of course, made that delicious meal last night and Arthur, well, you and Mrs. P. have him to thank for retrieving your overnight cases. In the absence of Agnes and Arthur, I am the chef du jour. So, how would you like your eggs? Fried, scrambled, soft-boiled, poached, shirred?"

Marjorie laughed despite the throbbing pain in her head and took the seat beside Mrs. Patterson. "I didn't know you could cook," she said to her fiancé.

"Just because we're getting married doesn't mean you know everything about me. Nor should you. A man must maintain at least a semblance of intrigue about him, otherwise his wife may get bored ... especially when that wife is you."

"I could never get bored with you," Marjorie assured him.

"Likewise, darling. Whenever you're around, I'm never quite sure what's going to happen—or who's going to be killed—next. That's a tough act to follow."

"I'm sure you'll do all right," she allowed. "So, what else do you cook?"

"Just eggs, really." He poured her a cup of steaming hot coffee. "Although I must say, I might only cook one thing, but I cook that one thing well. Right, Mrs. Patterson?"

The elderly woman swallowed a piece of buttered toast. "Mmm. They're wonderful. Light as a feather. You really must try some."

"See? Another satisfied customer." He bent down and gave Marjorie a playful kiss on the nose. "So? What's your pleasure?"

"Poached, I think, with runny yolks."

"Is there any other way?" He returned to his place behind the stove and set about boiling a pan of salted water. "I was thinking, darling. Why don't we enjoy a quiet day at home? I have some errands to run in town, first thing, but while I'm gone, you can spend some time writing your book and perhaps looking over wedding dress patterns with Mrs. Patterson."

"Oh, and we can decide on the menu for the reception," Mrs. Patterson added. "The ladies at the church league have submitted a bunch of ideas, but I wanted to get your approval, of course."

"Sounds like a capital idea, Mrs. P.," Creighton said approvingly. "And then, for dinner, Marjorie—if you feel like it of course—maybe you can make some of those lamb chops you made last week. They were quite good—especially with some broiled tomatoes from the garden. Mrs. Patterson enjoyed them too."

"Sure. You know I never mind cooking for you," Marjorie agreed. "I'll even make a raspberry cream pie for dessert—the shrubs bordering the woods were full yesterday."

"Mmmm, sounds good." He put two slices of bread in the toaster.

"Of course that's after we do some detective work," she qualified.

"I thought we agreed upon a quiet day at home." He cracked two eggs into the poacher and submerged them in the gently boiling water.

"After everything that happened last night you expect me to stay here and review recipes and patterns? We're close to cracking this case. We can't rest now."

"Marjorie, you almost did rest—permanently. Darling, I'm aware that we may be close to cracking the case, but we're also very close to our wedding day. It would be nice if you were able to make it."

"Oh Creighton," she pooh-poohed, "stop being melodramatic."

"It's not melodrama, Marjorie. I feel exactly the same way as Creighton," Mrs. Patterson expressed. "What if Detective Jameson is right? What if the killer intended to shoot you and not Diana Hoffman?"

"I think he's wrong," Marjorie asserted. "Diana was shot because she knew something."

"You have no proof of that, darling," Creighton challenged. "Just as you have no evidence that the killer, upon finding that you're still alive, won't come back and try to finish the job."

"But Creighton, darling—," she argued.

"Don't 'But Creighton, darling' me. I admit that you have a strong sense of intuition, and I'm even willing to follow it most of the time, but when that intuition could put your life in jeopardy, I put my foot down."

Marjorie remained silent while Creighton extracted the two poached eggs and placed them upon two slices of buttered toast. He placed the plate before her with a gentle kiss on the cheek. "I just want you to be safe, darling," he explained. "If anything were to happen to you, I don't know what I would do."

Before Marjorie had a chance to answer, Officer Noonan entered the room. His face was unshaven and he was clad in his dress pants and a white T-shirt. He stretched and scratched his potbelly. "Something smells good."

"Noonan?" they cried in unison.

"Where in blazes did you come from?" Creighton asked.

"The living room," he answered.

"Were you here all night?"

"Yeah. I camped out on the sofa. When I heard the girls were staying, I thought you might need some backup. Just in case the nut came back again." He pulled his revolver halfway out of its holster.

Marjorie stood up and gave the policeman a kiss on the cheek. "Thank you, Noonan."

"Eh, I didn't do anything," he rejected.

"Maybe not, but you were armed and at the ready," Mrs. Patterson said appreciatively.

He blushed. "It's still nothing. Hey, can a guy get a cup of coffee here? And maybe a couple of eggs over easy?"

Creighton smiled. "Coming right up," he obliged as he poured a large mug of coffee. "You want bacon and toast with those eggs?"

"Is the Pope Catholic?" He added three teaspoons of sugar and a healthy dose of cream to his coffee. "What's this I heard about lamb chops and raspberry pie?"

Marjorie sat down and salted her poached eggs. "I'm cooking dinner tonight: deviled lamb chops, broiled tomatoes, potatoes, and a raspberry cream pie. You're welcome to join us. Mrs. Noonan and the children as well, if they're back home."

"Nah, Eileen, Patrick Jr., and little Nora are with Eileen's folks until the middle of the week. And today is Sunday, my day off. We usually go to church in the morning and have our big meal in the afternoon. But since Eileen and the kids won't be around, I guess I'll open up a can of somethin'."

"Awww," the women declared as Creighton shook his head and rolled his eyes. Such a pitiful display he had never seen.

"Dinner from a can!" Mrs. Patterson exclaimed in horror. "How awful!"

"Yes, you must stay and have supper with us!" Marjorie declared.

"Really?" Noonan looked at Creighton through large glassy eyes.

Creighton sighed. "Yes, Noonan. Stay the whole day if you'd like. We can launder your clothes and hang them up to dry while you have a dip in the pool. Use one of my dressing gowns—robes—in the meantime." The Englishman slipped the policeman a surreptitious wink.

Noonan gave a subtle nod in return. "Pool? Might come in handy. From the looks of it, today's gonna be a scorcher."

Creighton cracked four eggs onto the sizzling skillet. "I believe the paper said it's supposed to be about ninety degrees today. A hot Sunday in late summer—sounds like a good day for swimming and lounging around. Come to think of it, why don't we take our breakfasts, coffee cups, and newspapers outdoors by the pool and the garden, while it's still cool enough to breathe?"

"What a wonderful idea," Mrs. Patterson agreed. "Come, Marjorie. I'm sure Creighton and Officer Noonan will refill our coffee cups. Won't you?"

"Our pleasure, Mrs. P."

"Thank you." The elderly woman escorted Marjorie outside with a sly wink in Creighton's direction.

"Nice work, Noonan," Creighton complimented when the women were safely outdoors and out of earshot. "Marjorie has no idea I'm going off to work with Jameson, and she actually seems to be looking forward to staying here instead of traipsing across half of Hartford County."

"I wouldn't be too sure about that," Noonan smirked. "Marjorie's not dumb. She'll eventually figure out what you've been doing all day and when she does—" He inserted a long whistle. "But don't worry. Emmy and I will try to keep her from flying the coop."

"Thanks, Noonan. I'll have you know, I never believed any of the bad things Jameson said about you," he teased.

"I wouldn't go that far if I were you," Noonan laughed as he refilled the coffee cups.

"I just have one question, Noonan," Creighton prefaced the issue that had been puzzling him since the previous evening. "'Emmy'?"

"Ah, my mother's name was Emmeline. My father called her Emmy for short. When Mrs. Patterson said her first name was Emily, I asked if she would mind me calling her Emmy." He shrugged. "She's kinda like a mother to all of us, ain't she?"

"Indeed she 'kinda' is," Creighton agreed.

Marjorie pulled a sleeveless navy and white striped sweater over her white linen skirt and plopped down in front of the vanity table. Thirty minutes had elapsed since Creighton had driven off in the Phantom, and with each passing second, Marjorie grew more suspicious of his activities. *Running errands, my foot!* she thought to herself as she ran a brush through her wavy blonde hair. *As if shops are even open for business on a Sunday.*

She applied a coat of red lipstick and checked her appearance in the mirror before journeying downstairs to the back patio.

Officer Noonan, covered by Creighton's too-long bathrobe, lazed in a lounge chair, reading the Sunday paper. Mrs. Patterson, wearing an old-fashioned Hooverette apron, sat in the shade of a wide umbrella, her collection of dress patterns, a list of recipes, and several sheets of tissue paper strewn about the table before her. “You look nice and cool,” she commented as Marjorie settled into an adjacent chair.

“I am, and yet I’m not,” the writer pouted. “In fact, I’m steaming mad.”

Noonan peered briefly over the top of his newspaper and then quickly immersed himself in the act of reading.

“Why, dear?” Mrs. Patterson asked innocently.

“Because I sense I’m being lied to,” Marjorie averred. “Where did Creighton really run off to?”

“He told you,” Mrs. Patterson maintained. “He had some errands to run.”

“On a Sunday? Unless he’s taken up selling Bibles, that story doesn’t quite wash.” She leaned back in her chair and stared at Noonan, her eyes burning a hole through the newspaper he held. “You know what I think? I think he’s out investigating the case. And you know what else I think? I think Jameson is with him.”

Noonan looked up from his paper, an expression of guileless naïveté on his face. “Detective Jameson? Why on earth would you suspect such a thing?” He faked a laugh. “You writers and your imaginations, eh Emmy?”

Mrs. Patterson tittered nervously. “Marjorie always was an imaginative child. I thought she’d outgrow it, but she never did.”

Marjorie leapt out of her chair. “Now I know I’m right! You never laugh like that, Mrs. Patterson, unless you’re ‘bending’ the truth. And, Noonan, the doe eyes look works for Shirley Temple because she’s seven, not forty-seven.”

He shrugged. “Can’t blame a guy for trying.”

“No, you can’t, but I can blame you for covering up for Creighton.”

"Listen, don't be angry with Creighton. He doesn't want you to get hurt—none of us do," Noonan explained. "That's why we kept you here and away from those people."

"I know, and I appreciate it," she acknowledged. "But I would have been fine."

"Pardon the way this might come out, but this is only your third case and yet it's the second time you've been shot. Two outta three may be great odds for a horse, but when it comes to the possibility of picking lead outta your navel, it ain't exactly good."

Marjorie flopped back into the chair. "You're right. If Creighton had been shot at last night, I'd be worried sick about him going out today too."

"Exactly," Mrs. Patterson agreed. "In the meantime, there's lots we need to do while Creighton's not around—like choosing a reception menu and then selecting the pattern for your wedding dress. I know the ceremony isn't quite working out the way you expected, but you can still have the reception and dress of your dreams."

"Yes, about the ceremony. I—" Marjorie started.

"Oh, Reverend Price didn't give away the surprise, did he?"

"Yes, he did, actually, and um—"

"I can't believe he told you. I so wanted to see the expressions on your faces when he substituted the murder bit at the end of the vows!"

"Don't worry," she assured. "Even with prior warning, I'm sure our jaws will still drop once the play opens. Just from the sheer ..." She struggled to find the appropriate word. *Wonder*! *That's it. I wonder how we got into this mess ... I wonder how anyone could think this was a good idea ... No wonder people elope ...* "The sheer wonder of it all."

"Yes, it should be lovely and lots and lots of fun too!" she gushed. "I'm just so glad you like the idea. I wasn't sure about it myself, but then I saw how excited Reverend Price was about the whole thing, and, well, you do realize, Marjorie, that he just thinks the world of you. The minute he heard that you were getting married, he started writing that story. Even if he wasn't performing the ceremony, he said he wanted to present you with what he had written as a wedding gift."

Marjorie felt a lump form in her throat. "He did?"

"Yes. He isn't exaggerating when he says that you're an inspiration." She giggled. "He told me he used to read Sherlock Holmes stories as a boy, but that nothing since then had given him as much pleasure as reading one of your books."

"Oh Mrs. Patterson," Marjorie exclaimed. "You have no idea how..."

"How much that means to you?" Mrs. Patterson nodded. "I know, sweetie, I know."

In truth, Marjorie was thinking that the elderly woman had no idea how much her words complicated matters. First and foremost, she felt extremely guilty taking exception to the Reverend's theatrical presentation. Secondly, and at a more intimate level, she wondered if, possibly, she wasn't making the situation more difficult than it needed to be. Perhaps she should simply capitulate to everyone else's idea of what she and Creighton's wedding should entail—yet, in her heart, she wanted it to be as she imagined. Precisely what she had imagined, she was uncertain, but she was positive it did not include a few acts of mystery-theater and a leaky carnival tent.

"So," she tried hard to remain casual, despite the whirlwind of thoughts whishing through her head, "what do we have lined up for the reception?"

"I'm so glad you asked," Mrs. Patterson replied with a sparkle in her eye that Marjorie hadn't witnessed before. "I tried to gather everyone in the ladies' church league together to compile a definitive menu."

"That sounds great. Let's hear it," Marjorie prompted.

"All right," Mrs. Patterson cleared her throat. "We'll start with punch—a raspberry lemonade, most likely, since raspberries are in season. I already spoke with Agnes, and she said she'd pick some of the berries growing on the outskirts of Kensington House."

"Oh," Marjorie exclaimed. "Should I not pick them for the pie? Will there be enough if I do?"

"I don't know," Mrs. Patterson replied. "I'm not sure if she's going to preserve them or if she's counting on a new batch growing in before then."

"Perhaps it's best if I wait until she's back."

"Mmm, maybe that would be best," Mrs. Patterson conceded as she glanced at the list she had compiled. "After the punch and the initial wedding toast, we'll bring out the sandwiches and canapés. I make a very good salmon paste; my thought was to put it on pumpernickel. You do like pumpernickel, don't you? Mrs. Montgomery makes a very good cucumber sandwich, but she volunteered to make curry chicken on white bread, heaven knows why! My thought was to tell Mrs. Montgomery that Mrs. Hudson—who volunteered to make the cucumber sandwiches, but happens to make an excellent chicken curry—is indeed going to make the chicken curry. And then I was going to tell Mrs. Hudson that Mrs.

Montgomery is going to make the cucumber sandwiches—this way it all works out. You understand, don't you?"

Marjorie felt her eyes glaze over. "Yes, I suppose so."

"Good. Mrs. Schutt volunteered her Perfection Salad."

"Of course," Marjorie responded. "I'm not sure how Creighton will feel about that one. When he used to dine at the Schutts', he witnessed vegetables floating in gelatin too many times to count. I'll have to warn him so that he doesn't run out of the parish hall screaming."

"It's revolting, I know, but I didn't want to say no, since she also volunteered her hot deviled ham canapés. If I said no to the salad, she might have pulled the ham from the menu." Mrs. Patterson placed her hand aside her mouth as if Mrs. Schutt was within earshot. "I have to be honest, I do enjoy Louise's deviled ham. I'm just dying to get her recipe. I asked her for it once, but it didn't turn out. I swear she left an ingredient out on purpose."

"I suppose that's what one does when she has a surefire recipe and doesn't want anyone else to swipe it." Marjorie second-guessed herself; in reality, she had been moving more toward combining the foods she had learned to cook as a child with the Cordon Bleu recipes Agnes had taught her. "I'm just assuming of course," she excused. "But if I had a recipe everyone wanted, I'd probably hold on to it like all get-out! Particularly if I were a Schutt."

"Hmm," Mrs. Patterson replied. "You're not far off. Mrs. Schutt is just the type to give a half-a—" She caught herself. "Half a recipe."

Marjorie giggled. "Were you about to say what I think you were about to say?"

"Oh no," Mrs. Patterson laughed heartily. "Well, perhaps..." She laughed even harder. "All right, getting back to business. Mrs. Reynolds is contributing her pimento cheese—it's terrible really, but she loves to make it. Mrs. Abernathy is making her mock crab salad. My opinion is that if you can't make the real thing, you shouldn't make anything at all. Sharon has volunteered her corn fritters."

Marjorie recalled the indestructible, indigestible balls of grease Sharon had brought to the harvest supper last autumn. "If things get dull, we can try bouncing them off of the Perfection Salad," she joked. "Whoever's fritter bounces the highest takes home Mrs. Schutt's deviled ham recipe."

"Oh Marjorie," Mrs. Patterson tittered. "You are terrible!"

"No, the fritters are," the young woman corrected.

"I know. I think they were the only thing at the harvest supper we couldn't get rid of. Fortunately, however, Agnes is making the wedding cake. That should be absolutely delicious, and it should make up for any other shortcomings."

Marjorie sat for a moment and considered the menu. "Mrs. Patterson, if everything other than your salmon paste, Mrs. Schutt's deviled ham, and Agnes's wedding cake is tasteless or revolting, why are we bothering with them?"

"Because it's what's done. Part of being in a small town like this is that we provide for each other—weddings, funerals, baptisms, any important occasion. It's what makes us a community."

Marjorie frowned and contemplated that statement. All her life she had done what was expected, what was "right." Now that it was her wedding day, she began to question this system. Why, on one of the most important days of her life, should she be eating someone's greasy corn fritters, or "mock" anything? Who dictated long ago that she, as the bride, shouldn't, or couldn't, make enough chicken fricassee to feed a crowd and invite the entire town and its neighboring regions for a feast? Better yet, why not allow Creighton the opportunity to have the whole community to Kensington House for a cocktail party by the pool? She didn't want, nor expect, anyone to provide for her wedding—if anything, she was more than happy to supply what was needed for the party. The problem was pride. Both on the part of the elder townsfolk who refused to break with tradition, and Marjorie who refused to let her fellow citizens think badly of her newly found "cosmopolitan" ways.

Marjorie forced a smile. By hook or by crook she was going to get through this graciously. Not that the experience was by any means a sacrifice, but Marjorie understood that most of the families contributing toward the wedding didn't have much for themselves or their families. For them to donate even a platter of sandwiches made Marjorie feel as though she were taking the food from their mouths. This sense of pride, however, was how 1930s New England towns survived the Depression in spite of the economic hardships of closed mills, bad weather, and unemployment.

"I understand, Mrs. Patterson. You know I don't want to hurt anyone's feelings. I . . . well, I just feel funny about all these folks contributing their time and money, especially when it's such a precious commodity these days. Creighton has so much and he'd like to share it—"

"I know he would, Marjorie," Mrs. Patterson flashed a knowing smile. "But for you and Creighton to give to them on a day when they should be giving to you would just about kill them. They don't have much left other than pride."

Marjorie blinked back her tears. "I know they don't."

"Enough talk of unhappiness," Mrs. Patterson ordered. "The only thing we've yet to arrange is your wedding dress. And I've saved this part for last because it's my favorite." The elderly woman cupped Marjorie's face in her hands. "Oh Marjorie. You're going to be a beautiful bride!"

"An angel," Noonan spoke up from behind his newspaper. "Mind if I sit in for this part?" he asked as he rose from the lounge chair.

"Not at all." Marjorie patted the seat of the chair beside her.

"I find a man's opinion in these matters to be most helpful," Mrs. Patterson remarked. "My Frank always knew what would look best on me. We never had a lot of money, but every Christmas, he'd go out and buy me a new coat. Something smart and stylish that I'd never dream of buying for myself."

"Your husband sounds like a nice man, Emmy," Noonan judged as he scrutinized the photos on the pattern packages with a critical eye.

"He was a nice man, Patrick. Very nice."

Several minutes elapsed before Marjorie jolted upright. "Ooooh," she cooed. "I rather like the neckline on this." It was a sleek, sheath-style dress with slashed sleeves and a draped neckline, however the hemline was short.

Noonan handed Marjorie a photo of a satin gown with a scooped back and a long flowing train. Also appealing was the three-tiered veil of fine tulle, which was attached to a flowered headpiece.

"That is beautiful," she sighed. "Too bad we can't put that train and the back design on the top of the other dress."

"Don't be silly," Mrs. Patterson chided softly. "Of course we can do that. Dress patterns are all the same, really: two arms, a bodice, a skirt. All that really changes is the size of the resulting garment and the way those pieces look when sewn together."

Something in the elderly woman's words resonated with Marjorie.

"Maybe that's why they're called patterns," Mrs. Patterson expounded on her theory. "They look different, but the fundamentals are the same and repeat over and over again. Like people getting married, having children, and then their children getting married... come to think of it, life is all about patterns isn't it?"

Marjorie stood up, knocking the chair over behind her. "Mrs. Patterson, you're brilliant! It is all about patterns. All of it! It's all just history repeating itself."

"Well, I wouldn't say it was brilliant, but—"

"It is!" Marjorie exclaimed. "We see that the dresses are different and that's what our mind focuses upon. But if we look beneath the surface, they're actually the same pattern, adjusted and redesigned to suit the situation and the individual wearing it. That's all this is... that's all any of it is. One big pattern and all the components are once again falling into place."

Noonan raised a questioning eyebrow. "What else would you expect?"

"Exactly! I wouldn't expect anything less," she shouted. "Mrs. Patterson, break out a clean sheet of tissue paper. I'll get a pencil!" She hastened into the house, her eyes wild and her hair blowing in the soft summer breeze.

Mrs. Patterson turned to Noonan excitedly. "I might be wrong, but I think she really likes the dress!"

TWENTY-TWO

CREIGHTON PULLED THE PHANTOM into the dirt lot adjacent to the small police outpost on the outskirts of Ridgebury. Upon the Englishman's arrival, Jameson emerged from the station, stepped into one of the two black Hartford County Police cars that were parked there, and started the engine.

Creighton brought the Phantom to a halt at the rear of the building, exited, and slid into the passenger side of Jameson's squad car.

"Thanks for letting me tag along, Jameson," he stated earnestly as he shut the door of the squad car behind him.

"Hey, if some creep with a gun took a shot at my future wife, I'd want to find the culprit too."

"Hmm," Creighton grunted in agreement. "However, considering just a few months ago Marjorie was your future wife and I was the one on the outside looking in, I sincerely appreciate the invitation. Not many blokes would be as magnanimous as you are, if they were put in the same situation."

"Why shouldn't I be? I know you and I sparred for a while over Marjorie's affections and that she ultimately chose you. But hey, that's life." Jameson pulled away from the police station, and drove onto Ridgebury Road heading toward Hartford. "I don't harbor any hard feelings. In hindsight, Marjorie and I are probably better off as friends. She's beautiful and fun, and her Miss-Never-Say-Die escapades are exciting from a detective's point of view, but it's nice to end the work day and have dinner with people who don't want to hear about the clues I've unearthed."

Creighton nodded. "That's understandable. If I did what you did for a living, I'd want to forget about it sometimes too."

Jameson nodded. "A good meal, my favorite radio show, and a friendly, fast-moving parlor game. Now, that's living, Creighton. Nothing better."

"Sounds like you're quite comfortable with the arrangement you have with the Schutts." He raised an eyebrow. "What about Sharon?"

Jameson sighed. "Sharon's a good girl. A bit spoiled, but a good girl. Not much of a looker ..."

"But a good girl," Creighton completed the sentence. "I get the idea. What about marriage? I know Sharon and her mother are keen on the idea, and you seem ready to settle down. If you're not serious about Sharon, you're going to have a tough time shaking her off. Especially with Mr. and Mrs. Schutt hovering in the background waiting to clear the nest of their last baby bird." The memories of dinners with the Schutts and Sharon's attempts at stolen kisses sent shivers down the Englishman's spine and a wave of nausea through his body. "Believe me, Jameson, I know from experience. They're the eagles and you're the carrion caught in their talons, just waiting to be deposited in Sharon's hungry beak."

Jameson glanced at the Englishman. "That's, um, quite the analogy there."

"I know, I think Marjorie's rubbing off on me." He rubbed his chin in contemplation. *Hmmm, perhaps the Reverend is right. Maybe I should try my hand at writing…*

"To tell the truth," Jameson confessed, "Sharon isn't that bad. I just wish she'd fix herself up a bit and maybe hang around people her age instead of her parents all the time. She could use a girlfriend, someone a bit more polished and sophisticated. Someone like Marjorie, for instance."

Creighton laughed harder than he had ever laughed in his life. "Friends? You're kidding, right?" He wheezed and gasped for air and then swiftly realized that Robert was completely serious. "Oh, um, er, sorry Jameson. I thought you were making a joke."

"No, I'm not joking. Sharon needs to see that there's more to life than what goes on right outside her front door. I think Marjorie could help her with that."

"I don't doubt that she could," Creighton answered. "But in case you hadn't noticed, Sharon isn't what I'd call 'keen' on Marjorie. And for her part, Marjorie isn't exactly enamored with Sharon either."

"I think a large part of that is because Sharon is a bit jealous of Marjorie." Jameson pulled a face. "All right, more than a bit—frankly, she's green to the gills. That's why she acts the way she does."

"Well, there's not much Marjorie or I can do about that. That's up to Sharon to change."

"Yes, it is, but I think Marjorie asking Sharon to be her maid of honor is a great way to turn things around."

"Maid of honor?" Creighton repeated. "Where did you hear that?"

"Mrs. Schutt told me. She hasn't mentioned anything to Sharon yet, but I think it's a swell idea."

"Yeeeeees." He dragged the word out in hopes that he might think of something to say that would bring this conversation to a screeching halt.

Jameson looked at Creighton out of the corner of his eye. "Mrs. Schutt didn't hear incorrectly, did she? Marjorie is planning on Sharon being her maid of honor, right?"

"Yeeeeeees and nooooooo . . . you know how fickle women are . . ."

"Yeah, I know, but I hope she doesn't change her mind. I think it would mean a lot to Sharon if she and Marjorie could become friends, and it would definitely mean the world to me. After all, I consider us good pals, Creighton."

Creighton was nonplussed. "You do?"

"Yeah, don't you? I mean, a fellow doesn't ask just anyone to be the best man at his wedding."

"They don't?"

"No." Jameson reached over and patted Creighton on the back. "I'm sorry, I surprised you there. Mrs. Schutt told me the news. I know you have too much style and class to ask such a thing in the middle of a murder investigation. So I'll save you the trouble and say that I'd be honored to stand up for you at your wedding."

"She did? I do? You would?" Creighton's voice went up half an octave, but he quickly recovered. "Yes, well, um, Marjorie and I were considering it, but our plans aren't final, mind you."

"Oh, you don't have to explain. I know Marjorie has to give everything the okay before you can make it official." He sighed. "I just wish Marjorie and Sharon were as good of friends as we are."

Creighton stifled a laugh. "Well, um ... I'll run the idea past her, but I can't make any promises. I know the idea of Sharon being the maid of honor came up in conversation, but I don't think it was definite."

"I understand. It's tough enough to pin Marjorie down on anything that isn't crime- or writing-related. But when you throw a couple of corpses into the mix and add in the fact that she's being shot at, all the wedding plans go out the window. Right?"

"Mmmm ... right ..." Creighton answered reluctantly. "So, um, do you really think Marjorie was the target last night?"

"Of course," Jameson replied arrogantly. "Marjorie's good at detective work, but a lot of people just see her as a nosey broad. Not that I'm one of those people," Jameson qualified.

"Didn't think you were."

"But when someone's wife is getting dug up because you're looking into his past, you can't blame the guy for wanting to bump you off. No offense against Marjorie, of course."

"None taken." Creighton tilted his hat forward in an effort to shield his eyes from the hot summer sun. "From that statement alone, am I to assume you think Trent Taylor is our culprit?"

"It was a bit transparent, wasn't it?" Jameson smiled.

"Just the part about digging up his wife," Creighton grinned.

"Yeah, that pretty much sums it up though. Trent Taylor had the most to lose if Veronica Carter stayed alive, and he also had the most to gain from her death. Not to mention his behavior indicates that he may have murdered his wife. You and Marjorie said yourselves that he was in a black mood over this exhumation order."

"Black and stormy," Creighton agreed. "However, I'm not convinced that Marjorie was the intended target of the shooting. I'll err on the side of caution and keep her out of the fray for now, but I can't shake the image of Diana Hoffman standing on my doorstep last night. The Diana who showed up at Kensington House was completely different from the Diana who Marjorie and I interviewed the other morning. The Diana Hoffman we first met was tough, confident, brazen even, but last night she had been reduced to a mere shadow of her former self. Something, or someone, had rattled her nerves."

"Well, we'll do a search of her apartment and see if we can dig up anything 'rattle worthy.' In the meantime, my nose tells me that Trent Taylor is our guy. He left shortly before Diana arrived. It's possible he hung around a while longer. Diana came by, they spoke, and judging by how wound-up he was at your place, he may have told her about his wife's body. Hell, he may have even confessed to murdering Veronica Carter."

"That's a scenario I hadn't considered. Diana obviously knew something that she couldn't, or wouldn't tell us. The Trent theory fits the facts as we understand them—but what about Diana's reluctance to tell us what she had learned? If she did know something about Trent Taylor, would she have felt obligated to discuss it with him first? Especially if we assume she had only seen him a few seconds prior to ringing the doorbell?"

"He might have said something that 'clicked' afterward," Jameson suggested.

"All right," Creighton allowed. "But what about feeling as though she needed to think it over? Does that fit with female psychology? Would a woman like Diana Hoffman even consider protecting a man who had once jilted her? Moreover, would she consider protecting the man she believed murdered her closest friend?" Creighton shook his head. "Your money may be on Trent Taylor. However, my money's on Marjorie sorting this mess out for us. No offense to your brilliant detecting skills, of course."

"Naturally," Jameson smiled amicably.

"Indubitably," Creighton concurred.

"Only, Marjorie's not here," Jameson pointed out.

"Since when has that stopped her?" Creighton challenged.

"Hmmmm," the men mused simultaneously.

Marjorie sat at the patio table, flanked on one side by Mrs. Patterson and, on the other, Officer Noonan. Wild-eyed, she grabbed a sheet of tissue paper and wrote upon it, in large penciled letters: *PATTERNS.*

Mrs. Patterson clapped her hands excitedly. "Oh goodie! Now you have to trace the templates for the bodice of the first gown, following the set of lines and guides for your size, of course."

Marjorie patted Mrs. Patterson on the hand. "I'm sorry, dear, but we're not working on those kind of patterns right now. However, I guarantee that once we start, you'll have just as much fun with this as you would with those dress patterns."

Mrs. Patterson pulled a face. "If you say so."

"I do say so," Marjorie continued, "because you're the inspiration for this. It was your comment that opened my eyes to what's been bothering me in this case. Namely, that it's all just a series of overlaying patterns. A tangle of patterns and history repeating itself... if we can grab hold of the correct pattern, we can trace it back to the source."

Noonan's brow furrowed. "Huh?"

Marjorie smiled. "Sorry, I got ahead of myself. For now, let's just note the patterns we see in the case—the incidents and themes that seem to have repeated themselves." She drew the number one on the paper. "For example, the first thing that struck me about this case is that this was Veronica Carter's second affair with a married man. The first was with Trent Taylor and this one was with Michael Barnwell."

She wrote the words *two men* beside the number one and beneath it listed each man's name as a separate line. "Neither man was happy with his wife, but neither was willing to consider divorce as a means out of the marriage." She wrote the names of Cynthia Taylor and Elizabeth Barnwell beside their respective spouses.

"And neither of them seemed too keen on the idea of marrying Veronica Carter," Noonan noted.

"Very good," Marjorie stated approvingly. "That's an excellent point you just made." She wrote Veronica Carter's name to the right of and between those of the two couples, with a large ">" linking her to both sets of names. "Here's where it starts getting confusing. The first marriage, and subsequently the affair, ended with the death of Cynthia Taylor." She drew a line through the woman's name.

"And the second affair ended with the death of Veronica Carter," Noonan inserted.

"Which is the murder that started this whole mess." Instead of crossing out Veronica's name, she drew a circle around it.

"Unless Cynthia Taylor's autopsy shows that she was murdered too," Noonan interjected. "Then that would make her murder the one that started this whole mess."

"Yes, that would change everything, wouldn't it?" Marjorie mused. "Without that information, I'm afraid we can't go much further with pattern number one, can we?" She drew a large number two on the page. "Next up, the two sets of friends. Michael Barnwell and Gordon Merchant, and Veronica Carter and Diana Hoffman. Gordon Merchant is in love with Michael's wife, Elizabeth." She drew a line from Elizabeth's name to Gordon's.

Mrs. Patterson spoke up, "And I overheard Creighton saying that Diana Hoffman and Trent Taylor were an item until Veronica came along."

"Indeed they were," Marjorie confirmed and drew a line between Trent's name and Diana's.

"Hmm," Noonan said meditatively. "When you look at the whole friend setup, you can see that Barnwell and Veronica were kinda playing the same part, weren't they?"

"You have a point, Patrick. Gordon might have been a better match for Elizabeth and Diana might have been a better match for Trent, but Michael and Veronica really cast a spell," Mrs. Patterson expounded on the officer's observations. "Without even intending to, they kept those couples apart. Sad in a way, isn't it?"

The trio was silent for a few moments.

"Speaking of sad," Marjorie segued, "there's also the two children fathered by Michael Barnwell." She wrote the number three followed by the words *two children*. "Michael Jr. was his mother's solution for forcing Michael Sr. into marriage. And I think it's safe to assume that Veronica conceived the second child for the same purpose. It worked for Elizabeth, so why wouldn't Veronica believe it could work for her as well?"

"It's the oldest trick in the book," Mrs. Patterson remarked. "So old, in fact, that I'm surprised Miss Carter didn't use it on Trent Taylor." She chuckled. "She must have gotten smarter the second time around."

Marjorie and Noonan nodded in agreement and then stared blankly at the sheet of tissue paper.

"I can't come up with anything else," Mrs. Patterson admitted. "It's up to you two now."

"Don't look at me. I'm fresh out of ideas." He pointed to Marjorie. "This is Nancy Drew's party now."

"Thanks, but I'm as stumped as you both are. It's as if there's another pattern—a fourth one—lying beneath the surface, but I just can't see it." She shook her head and sighed noisily. "Why can't I see it?"

"Maybe you're just too close to see it," Mrs. Patterson offered. "It's like the crossword puzzles in the paper. I can spend hours trying to find the answer to a specific clue, but the minute I set the paper down and do something else, it comes to me. Same thing with jigsaw puzzles. I get up, get myself a drink, and when I sit back down, the right piece just pops into view."

Marjorie glimpsed at her watch. "It's two o'clock. I guess I should start in on dinner."

"It might help clear your mind," Mrs Patterson agreed.

"By the time I pick the green beans and the tomatoes, we might have those autopsy results as well." She headed toward the house to find a container in which to collect the fresh vegetables. "I just hope Creighton and Jameson have gotten further than we have," she called over her shoulder. "Otherwise, we're in a heap of trouble."

Detective Jameson approached the apartment door labeled *SUPERINTENDENT* and knocked loudly.

A man in a sweat-stained sleeveless undershirt came to the door. He wiped his mouth with a red and white checked napkin. "Yeah?"

Jameson flashed his badge. "Detective Robert Jameson, Hartford County Police. And this is my associate, Creighton Ashcroft. We need to access Diana Hoffman's apartment on a police matter."

"Go on up and knock," the man shooed them away and started closing the door. "She should be home now."

Creighton acted quickly and stopped the door with his foot. "She isn't home. She's on a slab in the morgue with a tag on her toe."

"Dead, huh? That would explain why she didn't answer when I went up looking for the rent. I thought she was trying to stiff me."

"I assure you, the only person who's been 'stiffed' is Miss Hoffman... although not quite in the sense you meant it," Creighton stated.

"Okay." The superintendent held up a stubby finger. "One minute while I get the key."

Jameson and Creighton stood in the stifling hot hallway listening to the screams of young children, the shouts of arguing husbands and wives, and a myriad of radio programs all vying for attention.

The superintendent returned and led them up the rickety stairs to the third floor, where the stench of overripe trash combined with the aroma of potatoes being roasted over open coals.

The superintendent, who introduced himself as "Tony," slipped a key into the door of Diana Hoffman's apartment and, after much jiggling of the handle, managed to gain admittance. "Say, can you guys help me get the rent Miss Hoffman owes me?" he asked before making his way back downstairs.

"I'm afraid not," Jameson explained. "You'll have to contact her family for that."

"Oh." The superintendent headed back toward the stairs. As he did so, Creighton heard him mutter under his breath, "Can't get my rent... never around when you need them... what good are these guys anyways... ?"

"I must say, Jameson, I don't think I've ever searched a dead person's apartment before," Creighton declared. "What precisely are we looking for, and how do we set about finding it?"

"We're looking for anything that might tell us why Diana Hoffman was killed. Unfortunately, it could be anywhere, but, from my vast experience with the Hartford County Police, I can tell you it won't be out in the open. So leave no stone unturned."

"I won't. You know, I was a Boy Scout as a lad."

"Boy Scout?" Jameson repeated in disbelief. "I didn't know they had those in England."

"Of course we do."

"Really? I bet it's different than the Scouts here though. We give badges for camping and tying knots. What do they do in England? Give badges for the best cup of tea or the whitest skin?"

"Good one, Jameson." Creighton feigned a laugh. "Actually, it's quite competitive. We give badges for hiking, backpacking, shooting, sailing—the usual. The twist is that we name the three best in each category and then those three Scouts play a round of tiddlywinks to decide who receives the badge."

Jameson glared at him.

"Honest," Creighton crossed his heart and raised the first two fingers on his left hand. "Scout's honor."

Sensing that he had pressed his luck, the Englishman ventured into Diana's bedroom. Upon entering, Creighton soon realized why Diana and Veronica were such good friends, for they were both abhorrent housekeepers. The bed was unmade, the rug required vacuuming, or at least a good beating, and dust and cobwebs clung to nearly every surface possible—including the blinds, lampshades, and bedroom furniture.

Resting upon one of the nightstands was an open datebook, its pages turned to reveal Diana's appointments for the previous day. Creighton picked it up and gave the entries a quick perusal: *12:30 p.m., Lunch with Aunt Elsie*, followed by what Creighton assumed to be Aunt Elsie's telephone number; *2 p.m., Doctor Douglas*, again followed by a telephone number; and *7 p.m., Work.*

"Uh, Jameson," Creighton called. "Remember how you said that clues are seldom out in the open? Is that a hard and fast rule, or are there sometimes exceptions?"

Jameson entered the bedroom. "What are you babbling about?"

"This." Creighton held the book out for Jameson's expert opinion.

"Looks like an appointment book," was all the detective could muster.

"Thanks, Jameson," Creighton replied glibly. "That was possibly the single most profound analysis since General Custer looked over the Bighorn Mountains and said, 'Gee, I think some Indians are headed this way.'"

"What do you want me to say? It's obviously an appointment book with some stuff written into it."

"Yes, but what stuff?" Creighton quizzed. "Did you look at yesterday's entries?" He indicated the appointment written in for two o'clock.

"'Doctor Douglas,'" Jameson read. "Diana had a doctor's appointment. So what?"

"So, we saw Diana the day before yesterday and she was fine. Fit as a fiddle and nerves properly wound. When Marjorie and I left her, she was leaving for work. Odds are, she didn't do much afterwards."

"Okay, but I'm not quite following what you're saying," Jameson assured.

Creighton sighed. "I'm saying that Diana was fine when we left her on Friday. Yesterday, however, is a completely different story. She was rattled, nerves shot to hell."

"Meaning?"

"Meaning that something transpired between the time we saw Diana on Friday and when she showed up at Kensington House last night. And, with all due respect, I highly doubt that lunch with Aunt Elsie would have been that upsetting of an experience. Unless, of course, Aunt Elsie served Perfection Salad." Creighton grinned and then thought better of it. "Oh, I'm sorry, Jameson. I—um—I forgot that you like Mrs. Schutt's cooking."

"I do like her cooking," Jameson confessed. "But Perfection Salad is the most wretched stuff I've ever eaten. The thought of the shredded cabbage ..."

"... the chopped pickles ..." Creighton recalled.

"... the bits of pimento ..." Jameson added.

"... the chunks of celery ..."

Jameson shook his head in horror.

"... all of them suspended in a viscous lemon-flavored substance and slathered with Mrs. Schutt's soupy mayonnaise." Creighton shuddered. "That would have killed Diana Hoffman right there on the spot."

"You've got that right," Jameson concurred. "However, this isn't a case of homicide by salad dressing. Diana was shot."

"Yes, she was. And I think her appointment calendar could give us some insight into what upset her so." He grinned, hopeful that his explanation made as much sense to Jameson as it did to him.

Jameson nodded slowly. "You call Aunt Elsie and ask if Diana was upset when she met her for lunch. Then call the doctor and find out why she was going to see him. I'll continue searching the apartment. And, uh, Creighton?"

"Yes?"

"Good job," the detective acknowledged grudgingly.

TWENTY-THREE

CREIGHTON REPLACED THE TELEPHONE receiver with a loud slam. "Bingo!"

"What happened?" Jameson inquired.

"First, Aunt Elsie confirmed that Diana was indeed preoccupied by something, but she otherwise appeared to be in good spirits. In fact, she went so far as to say she had an appointment at two that would probably 'prove that she was being silly.'"

Jameson pulled a face. "Prove that she was being silly?"

"According to Aunt Elsie, those are the exact words she used. So, I expressed my condolences to the woman and went about telephoning the doctor. At first, I was concerned that the doctor's office might be closed since it's a Sunday, but fortunately, Dr. Douglas works out of his home."

"And?" Jameson urged.

"I called, pretending to be Diana's husband, and requested a follow-up appointment for my wife."

"Good work," Jameson praised.

"Thanks. But get this: the woman who answered the phone could find no records whatsoever for a patient named Diana Hoffman."

"Well, how does that help—?"

"Ah, not so fast! On a whim, I said that my wife sometimes uses her friend's name when scheduling appointments—they're inseparable, do everything together, all that rubbish. So, I asked if the appointment might have been under the name Veronica Carter."

"And?" Jameson urged again.

"My hunch paid off. Not only does the doctor have record of a patient named Veronica Carter," Creighton grinned broadly. "But, Veronica Carter had an appointment with Dr. Douglas yesterday afternoon at two o'clock."

"Diana Hoffman was using Veronica Carter's name for a doctor's visit? Why?"

Creighton shook his head. "Don't know, but the woman on the phone said she and her brother would be in all day if Mrs. Hoffman and I had any other questions. I don't know about you, but I have a ton of questions," he added with a grin.

Jameson returned the grin. "Then we'd best get going and pay the good doctor a visit."

"Let me preface this conversation by stating that, for all intents and purposes, I am retired from the profession of medicine." Dr. Douglas wheezed. Bodily, the physician was thin, balding, and extremely fragile. Mentally, however, he was as sharp as a tack. He spoke in a soft, English accent. "Poor health has forced me to slow my pace considerably. Oh, I still have my license, and I still treat a few of my older patients—some because they won't consider changing physicians this late in the game and others because they don't trust a doctor who's younger than they are—you can imagine how rare those are. However, I don't accept new patients, unless they are in dire need of treatment, and I don't share patient information without the patient's express consent. It's a code of behavior that has served me well the past fifty years, and I'm not about to change it now. With that said, what would you like to know?"

"We're here to speak with you about Veronica Carter," Jameson opened. "We understand she was your patient."

Douglas coughed into a starched white handkerchief. "I'm afraid that question is governed by the last item of the aforementioned code of behavior, Detective."

"Does that code of behavior apply to dead young women?" he questioned. "Because both Veronica Carter and her friend, Diana Hoffman, have been murdered."

Dr. Douglas lit a cigarette and offered one to his guests, who graciously declined. "Those are certainly mitigating circumstances, aren't they? In which case, I will help you as much as I can without discussing medical diagnoses, prognoses, symptoms, or specifics—for those, you'll need to obtain a warrant."

"Fair enough, Doctor," Jameson conceded. "So what can you tell us about Veronica Carter?"

Douglas began to cough violently. With one arm, he reached beneath his desk and retrieved a small oxygen canister fitted with a plastic mask. He placed the contraption over his nose and mouth and opened the valve. With the other arm, he reached across the desk and snubbed the half-smoked cigarette in an empty ashtray.

Within seconds, a female sexagenarian of boyish figure and girlish demeanor appeared on the scene. "Reginald," she scolded. "You've been smoking again, haven't you?"

Beneath the confines of the oxygen mask, the doctor shook his head in the negative.

The woman paid no heed to his denial. "Those cigarettes will be the death of you. You've been diagnosed with emphysema, and you still won't give them up! You'd think a doctor would know better. Oh," she exclaimed in surprise upon catching sight of the male visitors. "I didn't see you there. And here I am rattling on. I'm Gwendolyn, Doctor Douglas's sister."

Ever courteous, Jameson and Creighton rose from their seats, causing Gwendolyn to blush and curtsey.

"Detective Jameson, Hartford County Police," Robert introduced himself.

"Creighton Ashcroft." The Englishman extended a hand in greeting. "Private investigator," he added for flourish.

"Oh! I would have thought you were movie stars, you're both so handsome. The kind of lads you'd see in the society pages of the newspaper. Newspaper … wait a tick! I know you," she pointed to Creighton. "You're that fellow we read about. You helped solve that murder in Ridgebury!"

"Yes I am," Creighton humbly acknowledged while Jameson returned to his seat with a scowl.

"Reginald," Gwendolyn exclaimed. "Did you hear that? This is the lad who solved that murder up at that big mansion."

Having breathed in his share of oxygen, Dr. Douglas pulled the mask away from his face and shut the valve. "Yes, I heard," he replied crankily. "My lungs are shot, not my ears."

"Please, sit down, Mr. Ashcroft," she gestured. "No need to stand on my account."

"Oh no. Please," Creighton urged as he pushed his chair toward her. "I insist."

Gwendolyn accepted with a silent nod and positioned her ample derrière upon the seat Creighton had just vacated.

"If you could tell us something about Veronica Carter, Doctor?" Jameson prompted.

"Ah yes... first I can tell you that she was, indeed, my patient. She first came to me two years ago after a minor medical procedure. It was late at night, and she was feeling poorly. Her friend found my name in the telephone book and called, asking if I would see her. As I said earlier, I don't accept new patients—haven't for years—unless they're in dire need of treatment. Veronica Carter was in dire need of treatment."

"Any chance you could tell us the nature of the 'minor medical procedure?'" Creighton requested with a winning smile.

The doctor smiled just as broadly and replied with a flat "No."

"There's been a lot of confusion between Miss Hoffman—who made yesterday's appointment—and Miss Carter. Could you verify Miss Carter's appearance?" Jameson asked.

"Certainly. Miss Carter was a brunette with brown eyes. She had a slender build and was pretty—in a coarse sort of way. The friend who brought her here was blonde—dyed as so many girls are these days—and blue eyed. She was pretty too, like Miss Carter, but softer. It was this blonde, Diana, who showed up for yesterday's appointment. I remembered her name the first time she was here because I found it ironic that a girl named after the goddess Diana was... well, suffice to say she was an attractive girl."

"A young woman named for the goddess of the moon should be attractive," Creighton prefaced. "Moonlight, however, can be deceiving, can't it? Which leads me to the next question: yesterday's appointment was made in the name of Veronica Carter. When was that appointment made?"

"Oh, I can help you there," Gwendolyn asserted. "I keep track of my brother's appointments."

"Ah, thank you, Mrs. . . ."

"Miss," she supplied sadly. "It's Miss Douglas."

"Not for lack of opportunity, I'm certain," he averred. "In fact, I'm sure there's probably someone in your life right now who thinks you're—how do they say it here?—the bee's knees."

Gwendolyn giggled like a schoolgirl. "Well, I don't like to tell tales, but there is a Mr. Richardson down at the butcher's shop who always trims my rump roasts at no extra charge."

"See?" Creighton exclaimed.

"Oh, what an extraordinary detective you are, Mr. Ashcroft," Gwendolyn said excitedly. "And do I happen to hear a Midland accent?"

"You do," Creighton acknowledged with a bow.

"Oh, I knew it! I once dated a boy from the Midlands. Sweet he was, and had dreamy blue eyes like yours too. I was fifteen and completely smitten! Then our family moved to Canada and I had to say goodbye. Brokenhearted I was, but then we moved here, to the States, and I found the American lads quite exciting—a nice diversion for a little while—but, you know, I never could forget him."

"That's quite the story," Creighton commented. "Now, tell me, Miss Douglas, when did you receive the call from Veronica Carter scheduling an appointment for two o'clock yesterday afternoon?"

"Oh, that's easy," Gwendolyn replied with a wave of the hand. "It was the day before yesterday. What was that? Friday afternoon?"

"Did Miss Carter say why she wanted the appointment?"

"No. Nor did I ask. Patients sometimes think it impolite if I ask, so I scheduled the appointment and that was that."

"So this woman didn't ask any questions or say anything unusual?"

Gwendolyn thought for a moment. "No," she answered flatly. "Why?"

"Because by Friday afternoon, Veronica Carter had already been dead for several days," Creighton explained. "Meaning that Diana Hoffman must have made the appointment in the dead woman's name."

"She did," the doctor vouched. "She confessed to doing so when she met with me yesterday. She apologized for the trickery and explained the purpose of her visit."

"Any chance you could tell us the purpose of her visit?" Creighton requested with a winning smile.

Once again, the doctor matched the smile and replied with a flat "No."

"Well, then," the Englishman grinned and nodded his head awkwardly, "I'd say we've taken up enough of your time and that we'd better be going. Right, Jameson?"

The detective rose from his seat. "Right." He pulled a business card from the pocket of his suit jacket and handed it to Doctor Douglas. "If you change your mind, or can think of anything else, be sure to give me a call. In the meantime, I'll work on that warrant."

Meanwhile, Creighton extracted a calling card from the case in his trouser pocket and handed it to Gwendolyn. "And if you can think of anything else regarding this case—anything else at all—you can contact me at that number."

The two men thanked the doctor and his sister and exited the office. Once they had shut the door and were safely out of earshot, the doctor said to Gwendolyn, "I remember that boy from the Midlands. Nice lad, but he could be a complete imbecile at times. Hmph . . . must be a Midlands trait."

TWENTY-FOUR

IT WAS JUST PAST five o'clock when Creighton pulled the Phantom into the long tree-lined driveway of Kensington House and brought it to a stop outside the kitchen door in what used to be the service entrance of the mansion. The sweltering summer heat and humidity had thickened into a canopy of dark, heavy clouds that foretold of the tumultuous weather ahead.

Creighton double-checked the roof of the Phantom to ensure that it was properly fastened and watertight and then jogged down the few steps that led to the kitchen. The aroma that met his nostrils was tantalizing.

"Hello, darling," he greeted Marjorie as she stood at the sink, peeling potatoes. "Hello Noonan, Mrs. P.," he acknowledged the figures seated at the table, snapping beans.

"Hello. Did you manage to complete all your 'errands'?" Marjorie inquired innocently, her gaze still fixed on the potatoes she was peeling.

Creighton approached from behind and slid his arms around her waist. "Yes, I did, except for one."

"You're lucky it was only one," she remarked. "I'm surprised you accomplished as much as you did. Businesses close early on a Sunday, if they're even open at all."

"Hmm," he agreed. "Still, it's a shame I wasn't able to accompany Jameson while he arrested Trent Taylor for murdering his wife. However, I told him you were slaving away on a fabulous dinner—"

Marjorie spun around, potato in one hand, peeler in the other. "Arrest Trent Taylor?" she exclaimed. "Wait a minute! Then you admit you were with Robert today."

Creighton held up both hands. "Guilty as charged."

"And now they're arresting Trent Taylor. Then the autopsy results—"

"Arsenic. Enough to have put the Pied Piper out of a job," Creighton explained.

"And Michael Barnwell?"

"He's being released tonight."

"Oh that's wonderful!" Mrs. Patterson proclaimed. "I'm so happy that family can be together again."

Noonan nodded. "Yeah, the little guy must have missed his pop."

Marjorie gave Creighton a brief kiss on the lips and headed toward the telephone. "We should call Elizabeth," she announced. "She might want to come home early to meet Michael."

"Um, I already called and gave her the good news," Creighton admitted. "I hope you don't mind."

"No, not at all." She returned to the sink and the task of peeling potatoes. "Out of curiosity, what was Trent's motive for shooting Diana Hoffman?"

"For now the theory is that he shot Diana by accident, but that you were the intended victim. However, that might change once we get a warrant for Veronica Carter's medical records."

Marjorie pulled a face. "Why do you need a warrant for those?"

Creighton explained the circumstances surrounding Diana Hoffman's meeting with Dr. Douglas.

"Let me see if I have this straight," Marjorie presented. "We met with Diana Hoffman on Friday morning. Friday afternoon, she calls Dr. Douglas and makes an appointment for two o'clock the following day under Veronica Carter's name. She meets with the doctor—for what reason, we don't know—comes here to tell us something, thinks better of it, and is killed as she tries to leave."

Creighton, having removed his jacket and hat, slung them over the back of a kitchen chair. "Yes, I think you have everything."

Noonan and Mrs. Patterson nodded in accordance.

"What could possibly be in those records that would cause Trent Taylor to want to murder Diana Hoffman? It just doesn't make sense," Marjorie thought aloud.

"I don't know," Creighton shook his head. "Doesn't matter much to Jameson. He still thinks this is a red herring."

"A red herring? You mean, despite Diana's visit to the doctor under Veronica's name, Robert still believes that Diana was killed by mistake and that I was the intended victim?"

"That pretty much sums it up," he confirmed.

"Oh brother!" she sighed in exasperation. "What did I ever see in that man?"

Creighton chuckled. "I only asked myself that for three months."

She smiled. "I'm sorry, darling, but Lord, once Robert gets an idea fixed in his head he doesn't let go of it."

"In his head, that's probably the only way Diana Hoffman's death makes sense," he shrugged.

"I know," Marjorie threw her hands up in the air, "but you can't ignore certain facts just so that your solution to the murder fits. And that's exactly what Jameson is doing. He's completely overlooking Diana Hoffman's visit to the doctor and focusing on me being the intended victim, when I wasn't."

"You're preaching to the choir, darling. It's obvious Diana learned something and it got her killed. Unfortunately, we still don't know what that 'something' was, and until we do, I doubt Jameson is going to change his mind."

"And you feel no compunction whatsoever about arresting Trent Taylor before we know the whole story?" she challenged.

"We arrested Michael Barnwell before we had the whole story," Creighton pointed out. "It wound up he was innocent, but if he had been guilty, and we didn't arrest him, he would have skipped town."

Marjorie nodded. "You're right. I know you are, but—I'm not convinced that Trent Taylor killed Veronica Carter."

"Darling, Cynthia Taylor was poisoned. That's an indisputable fact. If we look at it logically—as you always say—you'll soon realize that although all of our suspects had a motive for killing Veronica Carter, only one had a motive for killing both Veronica Carter and Cynthia Taylor. His name is Trent Taylor."

Marjorie sighed. "I know. I'm being silly about the whole thing, but something about it doesn't feel right. Perhaps Doctor Heller was right about there being two murderers."

"Perhaps," Creighton granted. "But what does that famous intuition of yours tell you? Do you truly believe that the murders of

Cynthia Taylor, Veronica Carter, and Diana Hoffman have nothing to do with each other?"

Marjorie shook her head solemnly. "No, I don't. I just can't help feeling as though this case isn't closed."

He stepped forward and pulled her close to him with a kiss on the forehead. "That's because I was a heel. I kept you here and away from the action."

"You only did it to protect me," she pardoned with a kiss.

"I know, but you would have been fine." He smoothed her hair back and held her tightly. "I would have looked out for you and—"

The kitchen door slammed.

Creighton and Marjorie looked up to find that Mrs. Patterson and Noonan had abandoned their spots at the table. In their place lay a magazine clipping and a note, written in pencil on tissue paper. Creighton glanced at the article and pocketed it then read the note aloud:

> Dear kids,
>
> Now that Marjorie is safe, this old hen is going home to her comfy chair and a cup of tea. Patrick's giving me a ride and sharing a light supper. Then it's off to bed. I'm pooped!
>
> Celebrate the end of the case with martinis for two … and only two!
>
> Thank you for a lovely weekend.
>
> Mrs. P.

"Oh," Marjorie exclaimed, "I hope we didn't make them feel like they were a third and fourth wheel. Maybe we should go after them."

Creighton held up the letter and pointed to the postscript:

P.S. And don't let Marjorie come after us!

After a quick shower to remove the odor of Diana Hoffman's apartment building from his pores, Creighton, dressed in a clean white shirt, trousers, a dinner jacket, and tie, went about lighting the candles on the dining room table.

Outdoors, the thunderstorm was in full swing. Streaks of lightning illuminated the evening sky, followed by thunderclaps that vibrated through the floorboards and the windowpanes. Indoors, however, the house was filled with the heavenly aroma of lamb chops, potatoes dauphinois, buttered green beans, and broiled tomatoes topped with cheese.

Creighton followed the aroma to a series of chafing dishes arranged on the buffet. He lifted the lid of each dish and examined the contents in succession. *Perfect*, he thought to himself. *But where, on earth, is Marjorie?*

Lightning flashed and the electric lights flickered as Marjorie appeared in the dining room archway, wearing the silver dress Creighton had given her during their very first case.

"That's quite an entrance," Creighton noted.

"You should have seen me trying to rehearse it," she quipped. "Noonan must have blown the fuses three times before he got the flickering effect right."

He laughed and kissed her. "You look as beautiful as I remember. Perhaps even more so, since I'll be driving you home instead of Detective Jameson."

"Who says you have to drive me home?" she said provocatively as he pulled her chair away from the table.

She smoothed the back of her dress and sat down.

"Why Miss McClelland, what are you implying?"

"Well, if the rain clears, we can walk," she replied innocently.

"Indeed," Creighton said with a skeptical smile.

He selected a bottle of wine from the rack beneath the buffet and extracted the cork. "This is a Lafite-Rothschild Bordeaux, 1924." He poured a small bit into her glass and awaited her judgment.

She took a sip. "Very good. Not that I have any idea what I'm tasting for," she giggled.

"You're tasting to see if you like it." He kissed her on the cheek and filled her glass and then his.

"Oh! I should serve up the food, shouldn't I?"

"Sit tight. I've got it." He dished up two plates and placed them on the table.

"If this tastes as good as it looks and smells, I might ask you to cook more often."

"My pleasure, especially if I can cook in a kitchen as big as this one." She sliced into her lamb chop and removed a bite-sized piece. "Back at home, I have to wash the dishes as I go along so I don't run out of room."

Creighton sat beside Marjorie and took a taste of the lamb as well. "Mmmmm, this is," he said with his mouth full, "possibly the best lamb I've ever had."

"It must be," she declared. "I've never seen you talk with food in your mouth."

He swallowed and then laughed. "Sorry. We're not even married yet, and already my manners are slipping."

"Don't worry," she excused. "I'll marry you anyway."

He lifted his wine glass and took a sip. "Say, since we're on the subject, why don't we get married?"

"We are getting married," she replied matter-of-factly. "That's what all the hullabaloo has been about lately, remember? 'What church will marry us?' 'What sandwiches do we want at the reception?' 'Will Jameson pressure Agnes into making a rhubarb filling for our wedding cake?' 'Who killed John Braddock?'"

"I know about all of that... except for the rhubarb wedding cake. What I'm saying is, let's just do it. Let's get married. However you want it done, we'll do it and sooner rather than later. I'm tired of kissing you good night and then coming home to an empty house, not to mention an empty bed..."

"If you're that lonesome, I can lend you my cat Sam for the evening. He snuggles beside me when I go to bed at night."

"He won't tonight, darling. Because you won't be sleeping at home—at least not if I can help it."

She blushed. "Why, Mr. Ashcroft, what are you implying?"

He smiled. "I'm implying that you never did pay me back for that dress, as you so passionately, vehemently, swore to do."

"Well, I just received an advance for my next book, *Mayhem in Macedonia.* I'll happily write you a check, if that will even things up."

"That won't be necessary," he assured as he polished off a bite of potatoes. "I'm certain we can negotiate some other 'mutually satisfying' arrangement."

"I can cook lamb chops for you once a week," she teased.

"That's a tempting offer, but not exactly what I had in mind. I was thinking more along the lines of something that starts with candles, dinner, moonlight, a bottle of Lafite-Rothschild Bordeaux, 1924, and you wearing that dress ..."

"And what, pray tell, does it end with, Mr. Ashcroft?" She raised a seductive eyebrow and took another bite of her lamb chop.

"Sunlight, coffee, two poached eggs on toast, and you wearing nothing but my dressing gown ..." He kissed her softly, longingly.

Marjorie felt goose bumps form along the length of her arms.

He gazed into her green eyes. "... and a shiny new platinum band on your left ring finger."

This time, Marjorie initiated the kiss, her right hand sliding from his neck, along his strong shoulders and down his starched white shirtfront.

When the kiss was over, Creighton looked beyond Marjorie to the living room window. "Hmm, looks like we might end up with almost everything we wished for. It's stopped raining and, if we're lucky, the moon might make an appearance. After dinner we should finish our wine and partake of our ... dessert ... outdoors."

"Mmm ... sounds lovely. We won't have many more warm evenings like these." She swallowed a forkful of potatoes and feigned innocence. "Only, I didn't make dessert. I thought we might need the raspberries for our wedding punch."

"No pie?"

Marjorie shook her head.

"Well, you're a resourceful girl. I'm sure you can come up with something to satisfy my sweet tooth."

"I'll do my best," she purred. "However, if the clouds clear, there is supposed to be a full moon tonight."

"Really? Then I'd better gather my strength now." Creighton gave Marjorie a playful kiss on the nose and then got up to place a second lamb chop and another helping of potatoes on his plate. "Speaking of moonlight," he prefaced, uncertain as to why the subject should surface at such an inconvenient time, "all those horrible boyhood mythology lessons came flooding back to me today. I felt like I was back in boarding school."

"Oh?"

"Hmm, Dr. Douglas was talking about Diana Hoffman and the first time she went to his office. The doctor was obviously quite taken with her because he referred to her as the goddess of the moon." He ate a bit of a broiled tomato and his brow furrowed.

"What's wrong?" Marjorie asked. "Don't you like them?"

"No, no, the tomatoes are fine. I just realized I'm wrong. The doctor mentioned the irony of a girl named after the goddess Diana—well, he didn't finish the statement did he? I was the one who brought up the fact that Diana was the goddess of the moon. Though I'm sure she was the 'patron goddess' of more than that."

"She was an excellent hunter," Marjorie asserted. "Oh, and the Romans considered her a symbol of motherhood."

"No," Creighton maintained. "Really?"

Marjorie finished her portion of potatoes. "Yes. Women used to pray to Diana for fertility and then, once they had conceived, they prayed to her for an easy delivery." A sudden thought struck her. She let the fork and knife slip from between her fingers and stared blankly into space.

"What's wrong?" Creighton asked.

"Dr. Douglas said 'it was ironic' that someone named Diana had … what?"

"He didn't complete the sentence."

"What had he been talking about when he made that statement?" Marjorie pressed.

"About Veronica Carter's initial visit. Diana Hoffman brought her in, late at night, after Veronica had experienced some trouble after a medical procedure," Creighton recounted.

Mrs. Patterson's words from earlier in the day echoed in Marjorie's head. "Did Dr. Douglas say what this 'minor medical procedure' might have been?"

"No," Creighton took a sip of wine. "He wouldn't say much of anything unless we had a warrant."

"His sister," Marjorie exclaimed. "Dr. Douglas's sister. You need to call her and ask her just two questions."

Creighton pulled a face. "What makes you think she'll answer them?"

Marjorie counted the reasons on her fingers. "One, because you're English. Second, because you're handsome. Third, because you're charming. Fourth, and most of all, because you're going to ask those questions in such a way that even if she doesn't answer them directly, you'll be able to ascertain the truth."

"Oh?" He gazed at his half-empty plate. "May I finish my dinner first?"

Marjorie laughed. "Of course you may."

"Thank you, darling," he replied appreciatively. "And our evening beneath the moonlight? I suppose that's been postponed?

"Only until you make the phone call."

"What about the wine? Can we finish that first too?"

Marjorie glanced at the half-full bottle. "We'll see."

"All right," he agreed, then added under his breath: "And there goes another '24 Rothschild."

TWENTY-FIVE

CREIGHTON REPLACED THE TELEPHONE receiver onto its cradle and headed outdoors where Marjorie lay waiting in a cushioned lounge chair, a glass of '24 Bordeaux in her hand, and her silver satin dress incandescent in the light of the full moon.

Creighton adjusted his tie and headed in her direction, wishing, hope against hope, that the evening might turn out as he had planned. But whatever ambience had been created at the dinner table, and was heightened—for Creighton at least—by Marjorie's seductive appearance and a beautiful Connecticut evening, quickly dissipated with the questions, "What happened? What were Gwendolyn's answers?"

Creighton sighed and sat beside Marjorie on the chaise lounge. She passed him his glass of wine. "Thank you, darling. A resounding 'yes' to both of your questions. Veronica's initial visit with Dr. Douglas resulted from an infection she developed after a backstreet abortion. According to Gwendolyn, Diana called the doctor when Veronica's temperature soared."

"Hence the reference to 'a minor medical procedure,'" Marjorie stated.

"But how did you guess?" Creighton asked.

"I didn't. It was something Mrs. Patterson said earlier today. When I told her that Veronica Carter was pregnant with Michael Barnwell's child, she replied by saying that she was surprised Veronica hadn't tried that ploy earlier, since it was the oldest trick in the book."

"Mrs. P. was right on the money. Apparently Veronica had been seeing a married man—Trent Taylor obviously—and thought that getting pregnant was a crafty way of getting him to divorce his wife and marry her. The boyfriend, however, didn't buy into her scheme. He gave her the money to 'take care of' the child, which she did. Of course abortion is illegal, so Veronica was forced to go to some quack to have the procedure done. Less than two days later, she became ill."

"So Diana took her to Dr. Douglas," Marjorie filled in the blanks.

"Precisely. The doctor examined Veronica and performed additional surgery," he took a deep breath, "just to stop the bleeding. He gave her something to treat the infection, but the doctor who had performed the abortion left her with such a large amount of scar tissue that it was impossible for Veronica to ever conceive a child again."

Marjorie clutched Creighton's hand. "The day we told Diana that Veronica was pregnant—do you recall how she reacted? She started to say 'I didn't think—' She never completed the sentence, but it all makes sense now. What she was about to say is 'I didn't think Veronica could have children.' That's the reason Diana saw Dr. Douglas yesterday afternoon, wasn't it?"

Creighton nodded. "And then Diana came to see us. Although I can't, for the life of me, understand why. Nor do I understand how a woman who supposedly can't conceive a child can suddenly become pregnant. It defies explanation."

"I know," Marjorie admitted. "I can't make head nor tails of it myself. Did Dr. Douglas make a mistake? He must have or Veronica wouldn't have been pregnant. And if he did make a mistake and Diana stumbled upon it, then why is she dead? Who could have possibly felt threatened by the information she possessed? Trent Taylor? We already knew he was having an affair with Veronica—he openly admits to it. The fact that he got her pregnant and asked her to have an abortion is upsetting, but hardly worth killing over." She took a sip of wine and placed her glass on the slate patio. "None of it makes any sense."

"Do we have to make sense of it tonight?" Creighton asked as he tilted the backrest of the chaise to a lower position and stretched out beside his fiancée.

"Probably not," Marjorie affirmed with a smile. "What else did you have in mind?"

"A bit of this," he kissed her passionately. "And a bit of that," he ran his hand along the length of her body. "And of course, there's still the issue of the dress you're wearing."

"Oh that ..." she giggled and threw her arms around his neck. "If memory serves me correctly, you bought the shoes too," she spurred him onward.

"You know, I do believe you're right. Whatever should we do about those?" He reached down, unbuckled the ankle straps, removed each shoe, and then threw them, one at a time, into the swimming pool.

Marjorie bolted upright. "Wait a minute!"

Creighton flopped backward in exasperation. "Yes, I know you loved those shoes and don't want to see them ruined."

"No, it's not that. It's Veronica. How could she be the body in the cellar when Dr. Heller determined she was two months pregnant?"

"Didn't we already establish that Dr. Douglas made a mistake?"

"If he did, why is Diana Hoffman dead?" she persisted.

"I don't know, Marjorie," Creighton sighed. "All I know for certain is that at this rate, you and I will never have any offspring either."

"Oh Creighton," she settled back into the chaise. "I do want to ..." she ran her fingers through his hair and kissed him passionately.

"Then do," he urged.

She kissed him again and then pulled back. "But something isn't quite right."

"I know," he sighed wearily. "Let's figure out what it is before I pass out from exhaustion ... or frustration."

Marjorie leapt from the chaise lounge and retrieved a sheet of tissue paper from the house.

"What's that?" he asked, his hair mussed and tie undone.

"We worked on it this afternoon—Mrs. Patterson, Officer Noonan, and myself."

"This was supposed to help you solve the crime?" he asked skeptically.

"It's better than spending my day in a Model T, following you and Jameson to heaven knows where," she pointed out.

"Indeed. Please continue," he urged.

"As you can see, from the beginning, this case has been a series of patterns. I tried to record the incidents where, as Mrs. Patterson put it, history repeated itself. This is as far as we got. See, we have the pattern of Veronica having an affair with two married men, the two sets of friends, the two potential lovers, and the two children of Michael Barnwell. That was it."

"You forgot one," Creighton averred. "Doubles. Lookalikes."

"What?"

"You and Diana looked alike the evening she was killed. You need to add a number four." He shrugged. "That is a pattern, isn't it?"

"Yes it is, and a very good one. I didn't even think of it." She added jokingly, "Funny that you should remember the other blonde who propositioned you."

"You two had blonde hair and a similar colored dress, but believe me, you were never the same type." He rose from his spot, grabbed the bottle of Bordeaux, and filled both of their glasses.

"Funny how men have 'types,'" Marjorie commented.

Creighton handed Marjorie her glass and clinked his glass against hers. "Mine is a certain green-eyed blonde."

She took a sip. "Did you always prefer blondes?"

"I had a few girlfriends who were brunettes, but yes, for the most part, I've stayed true to blondes, or as you would put it, my 'type.' However, I was always looking for someone who fit the 'type' and yet surpassed it. I think any man with an ounce of sense does."

"Hmmm . . . it makes me wonder what Cynthia Taylor looked like. Was she a slender brunette like Veronica Carter? Was Trent looking for someone who surpassed the 'type'? Or—" she cut off abruptly.

"Or what?" Creighton beseeched. "Or what, darling?"

Marjorie appeared to be in a trance. "What are the Barnwells doing tonight?"

"Most likely what I wish we were doing," he quipped.

Marjorie turned and glared at him.

"Sorry, darling. Elizabeth mentioned that she, Michael, and the baby were leaving tomorrow on a cruise to Bermuda. Her parents were helping to pay the way."

"Bermuda? That's not governed by American law, is it?"

"No. It's a tiny bit of England off the coast of the States. Beautiful area. Simply stunning for a honeymoon."

"Exactly what I was thinking," Marjorie confirmed.

"Really?" Creighton uttered in astonishment.

"Yes. Funny that they're bringing the baby along with them," Marjorie mused. She pointed to item number one on her list of *PATTERNS*. "Do you see a problem here?"

"Of course I do," he affirmed.

"Oh?"

"I'll, um, let you be the first," he begged the question.

"Veronica Carter had affairs with two different married men. The first, as we now know, resulted in the death of Cynthia Taylor, by poison. The second resulted in the murder of... whom? Veronica Carter? I don't believe that's the case. If the second affair followed the pattern set by the first affair, it should have been Elizabeth Barnwell who died. And she did."

Creighton stared, open-mouthed. "What do you mean? Elizabeth Barnwell didn't die. She came to you to find her husband, Michael. She went to your doorstep, with her son in her arms, and begged us to help her."

"On the surface, that may be the case. But let's review the facts. First, Elizabeth Barnwell arrives at my house claiming that her husband has disappeared. Yet, later in the investigation—more specifically through an interview with Mr. Sachs at the New England Allied Insurance Company—it's revealed that Michael Barnwell appeared at work each and every day that Elizabeth Barnwell claimed that her husband had been missing. Michael says he stayed away from home due to the discovery of Veronica Carter's body, but why not stay away from work as well? Wouldn't the grind of that soulless office be just as distressing as anything he may have faced at home?"

"Good point," Creighton applauded. "If Barnwell had been that shaken up by the discovery of Veronica Carter's body, he wouldn't have gone to work. He wouldn't have been able to. Heaven knows if anything happened to you, I wouldn't be able to function at the level required by the New England Allied Insurance Company."

"Second," Marjorie continued, "the address and the key. Why would Michael Barnwell have left them in his jacket pocket unless he wanted them to be found?"

"Michael claimed the address was in his pocket to give to Gordon Merchant. As for the key, he said he couldn't remember putting it back in his pocket, but that it didn't seem unreasonable since he is a 'tidy' sort of fellow."

"Oh, he's tidy all right," Marjorie stated, her arms folded across her chest. "I might have been able to swallow the story about the key, but Gordon Merchant told us that he already knew the address when Michael asked him to watch over Elizabeth and Michael Jr., and I believe him." She shook her head. "No, Creighton. Those things were given to us by Elizabeth Barnwell so that we could discover the body and set this whole thing in motion. The other purpose behind them was that we'd begin to view Elizabeth Barnwell, a.k.a. Veronica Carter, as a victim, rather than a potential murderess."

"Veronica Carter was pretending to be Elizabeth Barnwell?" Creighton nearly shrieked.

"Precisely. Let's look at the patterns. Veronica Carter has an affair with Trent Taylor; however, Trent is married to Cynthia. Veronica pressures Trent for marriage and Cynthia, a few weeks later, dies, supposedly of gastritis, but we now know it was from arsenic poisoning. Veronica proposes to Trent. Trent refuses. Veronica goes to New England Allied to dispute the claim and meets, in the process, another unhappy married man who can further her cause. The two of them plot against Trent Taylor."

Creighton ran his hands through his wavy brown hair. "Of course... Michael and Veronica. They were in league from the beginning."

Marjorie nodded. "Veronica and Michael plot against Trent Taylor. Trent Taylor, who allegedly threatened poor Veronica when she tried desperately to break free of his influence."

"It was a lie," Creighton said breathlessly.

"Of course it was a lie." Marjorie took a deep breath. "But it's a very romantic story—the married lover who murders his wife and yet refuses to marry the lover who had loved him so devotedly. And, of course, Michael Barnwell is easy prey. He believes his talents are wasted. He believes he's been tricked into a loveless marriage with Elizabeth. He believes he's destined for a fate far better than that of fatherhood and marriage. He believes his talent and knowledge entitle him to a life of privilege, which has heretofore eluded him.

"Barnwell is captivated by Veronica Carter," Marjorie continued. "She knows exactly how to play him, how to listen attentively, how to tend to his neediness. And Veronica sees a new life in Michael Barnwell. He's smarter than any man she's ever known, and to her that equals success, particularly financial success. If only he could get rid of the wife."

"And the kid," Creighton interjected.

Marjorie shook her head. "No, I think she wanted the kid. Otherwise, why keep him around? Michael Jr. was enough of an incentive to coerce Michael Sr. into marriage the first time around. Heaven knows what he could finagle Daddy into doing this time. Besides, since Veronica couldn't have children of her own, Michael Jr. was the closest she would get to providing Michael Barnwell with an heir.

"They enjoyed the affair, for a while," Marjorie visualized. "But Veronica wasn't going to play second fiddle to any other woman. And Elizabeth," she sighed, "well, Elizabeth, knowing no other way to hold on to the man she loves beyond all rhyme and reason, became pregnant again."

"My God." Creighton felt a wave of nausea pass through his body. "Elizabeth? His wife? He-he didn't. Did he?"

Marjorie nodded. "The face that had been battered beyond recognition. The hands and feet severed in order to prevent print identification. This wasn't the work of a madman. It was the work of a killer who was trying desperately to conceal the identity of his victim."

"But the baby knew that Veronica, despite the façade, wasn't his mother," Creighton inserted.

"That's the funny thing about children, isn't it? No matter what Veronica did, Michael Jr. cried. But men," Marjorie hypothesized. "Men have their types. And Michael Barnwell is no exception. Just as two blondes in two blue dresses look alike at a distance, two slender brown-eyed brunettes could even pass for each other—and did."

"That's why Elizabeth Barnwell didn't wave to Gordon Merchant," Creighton stated as he began to recognize what had occurred. "She didn't recognize him."

"You guessed it. And she didn't recognize him because she had never met him before."

Creighton wrapped his arms about his future wife. "When did you know?"

"I didn't know for certain until tonight. But I first suspected something was wrong when little Michael came to me instead of his mother. No matter the circumstances, a child should stop crying when he's placed in his mother's arms. I chose to ignore it, wanting to believe that Michael Jr. was upset by his father's absence and nothing more, but then, when we visited the Barnwell house, and Elizabeth couldn't direct you to the location of a clean glass. I knew that something wasn't quite right. But I couldn't imagine …"

Creighton held her as she sobbed, quietly.

"Elizabeth—er, Veronica—whoever she is, told me that their ship sets sail at dawn," Creighton informed.

Marjorie wiped her tears and sat up. "Where from?"

"New York," Creighton answered.

Marjorie took a glimpse at her wrist watch. "It's just upon midnight. If we telephone Jameson ahead of time and then leave and meet him on the way, we should be there before they are."

Creighton smiled and kissed her on the forehead. "Anything for you, Marjorie. Anything for you."

TWENTY-SIX

Marjorie, Creighton, and Jameson lay in wait aboard the SS *Reliance*, a cruise ship destined for Bermuda as the first stop on a transatlantic tour that included St. George, Bermuda; South Hampton, U.K.; and Dublin, Ireland.

Marjorie held the binoculars to her green eyes and tried to pick Veronica and Michael out of the throng of people scaling the ship's boarding plank. "I don't see them," she exclaimed.

"There are approximately 750 people boarding, darling, so we may not be able to spot them right away," Creighton explained. "Indeed, the local authorities have plenty of men positioned around this ship, so they might see them before we do."

"One thing's for certain," Jameson joked. "If Veronica Carter and Michael Barnwell are here, they'll spot you in an instant. A tuxedo and an evening gown at six in the morning on a cruise ship in New York Harbor?"

"What?" Creighton joked. "Are we underdressed?"

Jameson pulled a face.

Meanwhile, Marjorie continued to gaze through the binoculars. "Oh! There's a couple with a baby! Wait . . . no . . . she has blonde hair and he has a turban."

Jameson plucked the binoculars from her hands. "Give me those," he shouted impatiently.

"You needn't yell," she scolded.

Jameson sighed loudly while Marjorie rolled her eyes.

"Marjorie, darling," Creighton began, "why don't you—"

"Powder my nose?" she completed. "Creighton, darling, I was just about to suggest that." She gave him a quick kiss on the lips. "Let me know if anything interesting happens. You know where to find me."

"I certainly will," he agreed and kissed her. After she had left, he stretched and yawned. "I tell you, Jameson, when this case is over, I could sleep for a week."

"You're going to have to keep the idea of sleep on the back burner," Jameson told the Englishman. "Because they're here."

"What!" Creighton shouted.

"Barnwell, Veronica, and Michael Jr. just arrived and are heading up the gangway," the detective explained.

"Terrific," Creighton remarked. "What do we do?"

"We'll stop them on their way up," Jameson informed him. "It's easier to stop them before they 'officially' board, than to wait until after. Once they 'officially' board and register, there can be naval policies and extradition laws to deal with. Therefore it's better to nip it in the bud."

Creighton and Jameson moved down the gangway until they were standing directly in front of the couple.

"Mr. Ashcroft," Elizabeth greeted. "How very strange meeting you here. Did you know that Michael and I were taking a cruise to Bermuda?"

"Yes I did. You told me when I called to let you know that Michael was coming home. Only you're not going anywhere," Creighton commanded. "You're both under arrest for murder. Oops, sorry, Jameson. That's your part, isn't it?"

Jameson nodded wearily and flashed his badge. "Detective Jameson, Hartford County Police. I'm afraid Mr. Ashcroft is right. You're both under arrest for murder."

"Murder? Of whom?" Michael asked. "Surely you know by now that I've been cleared of the murder of Veronica Carter. They arrested Trent Taylor for the crime."

"Indeed I do," Jameson replied. "I was, after all, the one who signed your release papers."

"Yes, you were, weren't you?" Barnwell remarked. "My wife also informed me of the kindnesses you showed her and my son. Your goodwill won't be forgotten."

"Thank you," the detective said graciously. "However you're still under arrest for murder."

Michael Barnwell shook his head with a smirk. "If I've told you once, I've told you twice, I didn't kill Veronica Carter."

"We know you didn't," Creighton acknowledged. "The murder we're referring to is that of Elizabeth Barnwell."

"The murder of Elizabeth Barnwell?" the woman by Michael's side repeated. "That's ridiculous! I'm Elizabeth Barnwell." The dark-haired woman held Michael Jr. tightly in her arms. The toddler, however, paid no heed to the woman's declarations of innocence and struggled to break free of her embrace.

"Mama!" the child cried as he leaned away from Elizabeth Barnwell and sought solace from the female passengers who walked past him.

Michael took the child from Elizabeth and gathered him in his arms. The toddler immediately grew quiet.

Creighton and Jameson watched the scene with extreme interest.

"Listen," Michael Barnwell began, "I don't know what you're thinking—"

"We're not thinking anything," Jameson disclaimed.

"All right, then I don't know what you're trying to pull here," Barnwell continued, "but my wife is innocent."

"Yes, she is innocent," Creighton averred. "She's also dead."

"Dead?" Michael Barnwell laughed. "She's the one who came to you in the first place. She's the one who asked for help."

"Help?" Jameson scoffed. "This woman here went to Marjorie and Creighton so that they'd be witnesses to your scheme. You saw their names in the paper and went to them so that they could vouch for you and Veronica."

"Veronica? You're all delusional!"

"Are we?" Creighton challenged. "Were you aware that Veronica couldn't have children? She had an abortion years ago that made it impossible for her to get pregnant. Did you know that?"

The blood ran from Barnwell's face.

"That's right, Michael, Veronica had an abortion that rendered her sterile. You didn't know, did you? If you had any idea, you wouldn't have banked your life on passing your wife's pregnant body as hers."

Michael held his son and looked away.

"Michael," he implored, "I don't know what this woman promised you, but you owe it to your son to do right by his mother."

In a flash, Veronica pulled the little boy from his father's arms and pulled a pistol from her purse. She pressed the firearm to the child's head. "That's it," she screamed. "You try and arrest us and the kid gets it!"

Creighton and Jameson both put their hands in the air. The crowds of people boarding the gangway stepped back.

"Look, Veronica. You don't want it to go this way," Jameson implored. "Bashing a woman's face in and cutting off her hands and feet are one thing, but absconding with her child? There isn't a court in the world that won't hang you."

"Get back!" Veronica shrieked.

Creighton and Jameson did as instructed, however Creighton's eyes never left those of Michael Barnwell.

Meanwhile, unbeknownst to anyone other than the washroom attendant, Marjorie emerged from the ladies' room, her face washed and makeup reapplied. She headed toward the gangway but, noticing a large crowd blocking her passage, decided to head in the other direction.

"Silly tourists," Marjorie muttered to herself as she headed around the outer perimeter of the boarding deck. *I adore seeing new places as much as anyone else, but there's no need to get so excited that one loses one's head and does stupid things... such as congregating like sheep on the only way off the ship.*

"Veronica," Michael Barnwell pleaded. "Everyone knows what we've done. It's ridiculous to go on any further."

"Get away from my baby," she demanded. "Get away from him!"

"Veronica," Jameson tried to reason.

"I'm not Veronica! Stop calling me by that tramp's name. I'm Elizabeth Barnwell, your wife," she corrected with tears in her eyes. "I don't know what's gotten into Michael," she said to Creighton and Jameson. "I thought we'd be able to sail away and forget everything that's happened."

"If you are, in fact, Elizabeth Barnwell and you love your son as much as you claim, why are you holding a pistol to his head?" Creighton asked.

"Because I don't want Michael to have him. I don't want him ... to take my baby away." She began to sob uncontrollably, yet her aim never wavered. "He threatened to take Michael Jr. and live with that—that tramp!"

"Veronica!" Michael cried.

"Don't call me that!" she demanded. "My name is Elizabeth. Elizabeth Barnwell!"

"We know your name is Elizabeth," Creighton reasoned. "You're Michael's wife and always will be. Veronica Carter is dead. You're free and clear," Creighton exonerated. "You can walk away scot-free if you put down the baby."

"If I put down the baby, he'll take him and go live with that tramp. He'll take my son away!"

"No one's taking your son away, Elizabeth," Jameson attempted to reason. "Just put him down."

"Yes," Creighton added. "Put him down and tell us about Veronica and all the things she's done ..."

"The things she's done? Well, I'll tell you. You've heard of Trent Taylor, haven't you?" she taunted. "I know you have, because he's locked up in your county jail. Well, he didn't murder his wife, it was Veronica Carter all along. Veronica did it because she thought Trent would marry her if Mrs. Taylor was out of the way. But you know what he did? He dumped her the first chance he got!"

"Go on," Creighton urged, trying to bide time. "Veronica went to the insurance company and reported Trent, didn't she? She reported him for killing his wife."

She nodded.

"I must say, that was brilliant!" Creighton exclaimed. "But not as brilliant as Veronica's next trick: murdering Elizabeth Barnwell and then taking her place."

"Taking her . . ." she appeared to be disoriented. "But I'm . . ." she muttered before laughing uncontrollably. She spoke again, this time her voice stronger and slightly less refined than it had been. "That was good, wasn't it? Especially the part where I knocked on your fiancée's door and said my husband was missing. Michael had never been missing. When his wife told him she was pregnant in order to hold on to him, we agreed to kill her, but not like I killed Trent's old lady. This had to be better."

She laughed again. "Oh, we were good, but not nearly as good as my performance at your house. 'Goodbye, Mr. Ashcroft,'" she mimicked.

"It was good, until you crossed paths with Diana Hoffman," Creighton supposed.

"Diana was the only possible snag. She knew about the abortion and that I might not be able to have children. I was counting on her putting it down to a mistake by an elderly doctor."

"But then she saw you," Creighton surmised. "And she had to die."

"What else was I supposed to do? I worked hard—we worked hard—to make this all work, and we were almost there. If it weren't for you . . ." She turned the pistol from Michael Jr. and onto Creighton.

Seeing an opportunity to free the child, Marjorie emerged from her hiding place. She lunged forward, pounced upon the woman, and wrestled her to the ground, all the while barking orders. "Creighton! Grab the baby! Jameson! Grab the—"

Before she could finish, the gun went off and the two women lay lifeless on the ship's deck.

"Marjorie!" Creighton shouted, Michael Jr. still in his arms.

"Creighton?" a soft voice answered.

"Marjorie?"

"Creighton?"

Creighton drew near and grasped Marjorie's hand from beneath the dead figure of Veronica Carter.

"Darling, can you get her off of me? She's quite heavy," Marjorie explained calmly.

"Of course I can," Creighton laughed.

TWENTY-SEVEN

As Veronica Carter's body was removed from the ship and Jameson took Michael Barnwell away in handcuffs, Marjorie and Creighton basked in the glow of a brilliant New York City sunrise.

"What about Michael Jr.?" Marjorie asked.

"I had Jameson look into it before we got here," Creighton explained. "After all the trouble with Mary Stafford during our first case, I had a feeling you'd want to make sure he was protected—when I called Jameson and asked him to meet us here, I made sure he had Noonan check out the boy's relatives. He has aunts and uncles galore—on his mother's side—who are willing to take him in. Seems none of them liked Michael Sr. to begin with."

"You know, Mr. Ashcroft, I could go for a guy like you." Marjorie kissed him passionately, only to be interrupted by the sound of a ship's horn. Her eyes grew wide. "Oh no! That's last call—we'd better get ashore!" She took Creighton by the hand and led him to the gangway, only to find that it had been removed. "Now what?"

"Marry me, Marjorie."

"What?"

"Marry me. Here. Today. After all, a man can grow old waiting to catch you between cases," Creighton rationalized.

"But what about our wedding plans? The whole town is counting on us."

"We can take them up on their offer when we get back. Or do them one better by having the Reverend premiere his play at Kensington House."

"And what about Mrs. Patterson?" she asked. "She'll be terribly disappointed if we elope."

"Will she?" He produced a magazine clipping from his pocket and presented it to Marjorie.

"'The Benefits of Eloping,'" she read aloud. "'Why More and More Couples Are Tying the Knot away from Home . . . *Good Housekeeping Magazine, August 1, 1935.*'"

A smile spread across Marjorie's face. "Why, Mrs. Patterson!" She grabbed Creighton by his shirtfront, pulled him close and then gave him the most memorable kiss of his life.

"Is that a yes?" Creighton asked.

She threw her arms around his neck and kissed him again. "What do you think?"

"Why, Mrs. Ashcroft," he declared as the ship pulled out of New York Harbor and into the calm azure depths of the Atlantic Ocean.

Photograph by David Barnum

ABOUT THE AUTHOR

Amy Patricia Meade graduated cum laude from New York Institute of Technology and currently works as a freelance technical writer. Amy lives with her husband, Steve, his daughter, Carrie, and their two cats, Scout and Boo. She enjoys travel, cooking, needlepoint, and entertaining friends and family, and is a member of Sisters in Crime.